BREAKOUT!

Captain Manning was not a total fool. When he saw the black hole in the center of Steele's palm, he knew exactly what was happening.

It was just too late to do anything about it.

The 10mm pistol built into Donovan Steele's arm cracked. A blue-black hole appeared between Manning's sandy eyebrows, and the back of his skull and about two-thirds of his brain splattered across the side of the Cadillac Gage.

The lasers in Steele's eyes flashed ruby. They weren't powerful enough to harm a person, not even strong enough to cause retinal scarring. They were *plenty* strong enough to momentarily flash-blind the turret gunner, filling his eyes with gigantic green after-image blots and filling his head with the terrified conviction his eyes had been burned out. His thumbs contracted on the firing switches.

A burst of 40mm grenades hit the front of the house. A young lieutenant, manning an armored car outside, knew exactly what was happening: *breakout!*

FUGITIVE STEELE

BY
S. L. HUNTER

BERKLEY BOOKS, NEW YORK

FUGITIVE STEELE

A Berkley Book / published by arrangement with
the author

PRINTING HISTORY
Berkley edition / May 1991

ISBN: 0-425-12767-2

A BERKLEY BOOK® TM 757,375
Berkley Books are published by The Berkley Publishing Group,
200 Madison Avenue, New York, New York, 10016.
The name "Berkley" and the "B" logo
are trademarks belonging to Berkley Publishing Corporation.

PRINTED IN THE UNITED STATES OF AMERICA

10 9 8 7 6 5 4 3 2 1

To Bill DeVaughan
With thanks
For hospitality
and tutelage . . .

_ PROLOGUE _____

Driven by counterrotating black blades like carbon-fiber scythes, the verti fled west through the night.

The autopilot was an AI routine fully capable of handling the small craft from takeoff through landing, provided nothing too untoward happened. There was a Croatian weather satellite still functional that gave coverage of southwestern North America, and it showed no storm systems squatting atop the mountain ramparts that shielded the Rio Grande Valley from the ceaseless Great Plains winds. He rested his head against the seatback and let the trails of stars through Lexan crawl across his face. The tilt-rotor could fend for itself for a while without the aid of its human pilot.

Human. The word sounded in his head like a gong-beat of irony. The skull resting against padded plastic was covered in thick black hair cut short, and the features on the front were handsome in a rough way, beginning to show some signs of weather and worry and general abuse. But the skull was not bone. It was polymerized alloy, nysteel. What it contained was not a brain.

Donovan Steele sighed. It was an affectation; he didn't need to breathe, though he still was in the habit.

But then he didn't need rest, really. At least the physical part of him. His organic components did grow fatigued, such as remained—internal organs, reproductive organs, some bunched webs of muscle strung over nysteel skeleton. He could even eat and digest food to provide sustenance for what flesh and blood still comprised him.

But it was a gesture. A sop to a personality that had been downloaded from the CIA's computer files into the thing government scientists had built out of what an ambush by the Borodini mob had left of Lt. Donovan Steele, NYPD Special Operations. All that mattered of Steele was driven by a fusion generator in his chest.

He closed his eyes. They'd done quite a job on him, the Project Download scientists had. Sometimes he thought the flesh of him was all that kept him functioning. That contact with some remnant of his earlier reality, his earlier identity, kept him going through the tragedy and torment and the nightmares, the living fragments of other people's memories they had accidentally poured into the nysteel box that was his skull.

They made Stalker over even more completely. Steele's former partner, his best friend Mick Taylor, killed in the same ambush that trashed Steele—so Steele thought. But enough of Taylor had survived that they were able to suck his mind out of the wreckage and siphon it into a new-generation cyborg, an entity meant to resculpt the face of war: Stalker. Stalker had lacked flesh, and Stalker had gone mad. He destroyed the Project Download lab and went on a killing spree. Eventually he kidnapped Steele's daughter, Cory, and got her killed attempting to trap Steele. Then Steele killed him.

They'd left Steele a few rags of flesh to cling to. And Steele wasn't mad. Yet. Even if the government of the no longer particularly United States said he was.

They needed an excuse to hunt him like an animal.

He opened his eyes. He was wrung out completely, as if he were climbing a mountain with an armored Japanese subcompact strapped to his back. It was not a physical sensation. The accretion of fatigue poisons meant nothing to him.

He held up a hand, flexed the fingers. In the starlight and the gentle instrument glow the movement seemed fluid, the skin *natural. It would in bright light, too, or even under a micro-scope. But it was counterfeit. Polymer.*

A slight servomotor whine and the barrel of a 10mm pistol protruded from his right palm. He stared at it a moment as if unfamiliar with it, then retracted it. It was cool and dry in the cabin, and the wind rush and the murmur of the props in their barrel-shaped shrouds combined in a soothing white-noise har-mony. He would not be soothed.

He had his built-in pistol in one arm and a carbon-pulse laser in the other. He had a variety of other attachments which he could put on in place of his hands, "battle mods" and tools. They all rode in back, neatly packaged in nysteel cases and foam.

Do they define me? *he wondered.* Am I anything other than an appendage, a tool to be plugged in at need, or thrown away when it's no longer necessary?

He shook his head. He had no physical need of rest, but he had a more-than-human need of respite. Perhaps he should sleep. He wasn't getting the cross-talk dreams so often any more, since he'd actually met Donna Barrett, whose husband's memories had accidentally contaminated his own when his personality was downloaded into his artificial brain.

If only he could stop dreaming of the procession of the dead. His dead. Susan. Cory. Mick. Dev Cooper. Oliver Higgins. Linda Tellerman and Ice and Raven—filing by in a constant zombie progression, china eyes staring into him the accusation their dead lips could not frame.

You killed us.

He extruded the ten millimeter once more. He'd killed others too, scores of them, and for those he felt no remorse. But he'd had enough. It was time he left that all behind . . .

"Attention, please," *a synthesized voice said from the con-sole.* "We are approaching the Sandias."

He sat up, peered through the windscreen. A VCASS helmet hung to the side. His augmented eyes were more than keen enough to get him through the mountains. If he wanted, he could jack directly into the flight computer, make the entire aircraft into one of his battle mods. He was a versatile kind of cyborg.

He flipped up the arms of his seat, activated the hands-on joystick controls. "I'll take over for landing in Albuquerque," he said.

"Acknowledged." *He felt the craft come alive in his fingers as the autopilot routine surrendered control. Piezoelectric sensors gave him a greater than human sensitivity of touch.*

"Donovan, Donovan," *a voice said from the console.* "You can't run from yourself."

He grimaced. It was not the barely modulated imitation speech of the autopilot.

It was his own voice.

"I must be the luckiest guy in the world," *he said, voice rusty from disuse.* "My conscience actually talks to me from a loudspeaker."

"Who else can talk to himself without knowing what the answer will be in advance? At least you're assured of stimulating conversation."

"Matrix, you're a pal."

"They'll hunt you down, you know. No matter where you go."

"Look. Everyone I know is dead. At least I can try to find someplace where the ghosts don't crowd me everywhere I turn."

The verti began to rock as it came into the updrafts off the sun-warmed rocks of the pass. He grinned, enjoying the sensual feel of the agile little aircraft responding to his touch. "Shoot," *Dev Cooper had told him one afternoon when he was still hitting the bottle,* "if it feels real, what the hey? Evidence of the senses's all any of us have to go on, partner." *Sometimes he could actually live that.*

"Besides," *he said,* "I know you're always there looking out for me."

"That's me. A regular guardian angel." *A pause.* "Don't lie to me, Donovan. It's Los Alamos. You think they can give you your body back."

"So?"

Matrix said nothing, allowing his flesh and blood and nysteel twin to stew in the realization that the only answer he could come up with was adolescent defiance. Matrix had a habit of going Zen on him, did it more and more the last few months. It was a real pisser sometimes.

"You can't go back," *Matrix said*. "That's the other half of the equation."

"What, are you plugged into some kind of aphorism-a-day service online?"

"Very good, Donovan. Very adroit. You were always good at dodging. Except when the Borodinis set you up."

"Real funny."

"Give it up, Donovan. You can no more go back to being an ordinary human than you can devolve back into a tadpole, even if they by some miracle can give you your body back."

"If you're really me, why don't you talk more like me?"

"I'm moving on. Evolving. I've transcended the physical world—and if I can do it, obviously you can too. Come on, Donnie. If you're looking for a *meaningful* change, just jack in and I'll set you free. Really and truly *free*."

Steele rubbed his chin. He was discouraged, bone weary. But somehow he wasn't quite ready to become a pure electron flow like his "brother."

A few lights shone like tiny luminous insects down among the trees. In the year since he'd left New York there had been trouble in the still-settled area of the Southwest—trouble everywhere, in fact, as if the cyanoacrylate and string that held the remaining United States together were starting to pull apart. But it wasn't his *trouble. The dead weren't* his *dead. Maybe he could hold himself apart—he had fought so long and so hard, and all he had to show for it was blood and ghosts. . . .*

Red. He felt the plane die in his hands as impact/explosion drove the breath from his lungs. Furnace glare surrounded him, suffused him—are we on fire? He had no sensation of pain, just an awareness of losing control. Was that the world spinning around him, or was the verti . . .

Black.

1

The hands that fumbled at the back of her fake leather midi-corset top were not hands that had much experience with women's clothing. *Fuckin' figures,* she thought, and bit her lip hard to keep from screaming.

The chains that held her hands above her head were stripping the skin from her wrists. The dust and dirt in the derelict building were getting in the raw patches, and the fine gray volcanic grit that overlaid everything in the half-living city stung like salt.

Her captor grunted peevishly behind his black cloth mask. *Jesus, just tear it, it's only plastic,* she wanted to scream. Who knew what this crazy puke would do if he got frustrated enough? Sabrina didn't have much modesty, or she wouldn't have been in her current line of work. If he wanted to see her tits so badly, well then, let him.

She tossed her head to get the sweat-heavy strands of her bangs out of her eyes. He yipped and jerked back as her long blond hair whipped across his hood.

He stared at her. One of his eyeholes had slipped off true.

7

The eye that glared out the other was hazel and crazy.

And more than a little fearful, she thought. She'd been a psych student at one time; she'd been a lot of things. She might have a chance to be a few more, if she could only figure this right . . .

She lowered her head and smiled at him. Her eyes were big and wildflower blue. Because she took her decadence in measured doses, her eyes were unframed by smudges and bags, and her skin was creamy. Her lips said she could suck-start a Harley. They didn't lie.

"Hey there," she husked, way down in her throat. "No need to be so rough. I can make it good for you. Better than you ever imagined."

Ignoring the pain the motion sent knifing into her shoulder sockets, she rolled her hips. The pseudo-snakeskin jeans might have been applied with an airbrush, and the top button was undone—both for effect and because she'd put on a couple of pounds since she bought them over in the Republic of Texas. She was not a skinny woman, though she was a long way from being heavy, or even plump.

His hands were soft, she'd spotted that right away, as she was coming to the sensation of her weight being supported by her wrists and shoulders and her stomach churning from the lingering fumes of whatever he'd used to put her out. His right palm still stung when it connected with her cheek with surprising force.

"*Bitch!*" he hissed. His voice was muffled by the mask. "Harlot! Don't talk to me, don't dare talk to me!" His voice rose and broke at the end like an adolescent's.

Harlot? Jesus, nobody says "harlot" anymore. This is one sick puppy. Unfortunately, that wasn't news.

The toes of Sabrina's figured stockings smudged in the cement and volcano dust gathered on the concrete floor as the chain's torsion stopped her clockwise turning and began to rotate her slowly in the other direction. Her arms screamed in their sockets.

She bit her lip until the blood started. *No way I'm going to let this bastard hear me scream,* she thought. *No way.*

Her eyes were shut. She could hear his breath snuffling within his hood. She concentrated on her wrists, making herself feel them in detail despite the pain. She'd played at bondage enough to know that it's tough to secure a person's wrists with plain chains; skin slides on steel. And the blood gave lubrication. If she could just work the chain over the condyle knobs at the ends of radius and ulna . . .

She felt a kiss of cool against the skin above her navel. She looked down.

He had an archaic straight razor, a real museum piece. It was open. The blade was edge up, blunt tip resting against her bare belly. As she watched, he brought it upward. The bottommost of the laces that held the front halves of her top a handsbreadth apart parted with a pop that sounded like thunder in the afternoon stillness. Or was that the roaring in her ears?

She knew then that she had lied to herself.

He was going to hear her scream.

Jilly Romero wasn't used to being a slave. But then she wasn't intending to stay one.

She dabbed forehead sweat with the back of her hand. The terrycloth headband Elder Brother Banner had thoughtfully allowed her was supersaturated now and starting to drip. The evaporative cooling effect was overmatched by the way the salt sweat stung when it rolled into her eyes.

She pulled another tough green stalk tipped with yellow-dot buds from the turned earth of the vegetable garden. Thank god Russian thistle didn't start to turn hard and, well, *thistly* until it reached its growth and started to dry out. She'd rip her fingers to shreds; the Stewards of the Church of Christ in Living Color thought adversity strengthened the soul, which meant wearing work gloves weakened it—that was the kind of syllogism their feeble minds came up with. Besides, she was powerfully allergic to the weeds when they reached that stage.

It was kind of high up in the Upper Sonoran lifezone for tumbleweeds to grow, here in the Manzano foothills overlooking the shattered sprawl of Albuquerque. But they were tenacious bastards, and imperialistic to boot, always trying to extend their reach, like the piñon scrub the work gangs were always having to hack back.

Then again, the world had been turned upside-down since the Eruption. Maybe the Durga-Dancers had it right after all. What a pisser *that* would be.

Risking rebuke and a quick lick from the riding crops the

Lay Brothers and Sisters carried to keep the minds of slaves
and acolytes on doing God's work, she sat up straight for a
moment, rump on heels. She was an olive-colored young
woman, starting to burn brown on the areas exposed to the
ferocious spring sun, medium height, with heavy blue-black
hair worn in bangs in front and a thick ponytail down her back.
It was a privilege to be allowed to keep her hair, as the Lay
Sisters in charge of the female slaves loved to remind her. The
male slaves had their heads shaved. But the Eldest Brother
believed in women wearing their hair long.

*At least I'm not going to have to worry about my fat ass
anymore,* she thought—most people wouldn't have said she
was *fat* at all, but she was just going through the transition
from notably gawky adolescent to young woman, and wasn't
entirely used to the filling-out process. *Eldest Brother must like
'em skinny, too, to judge by what they feed us.* She was glad
for the bulky work clothes she wore, though they were stifling
on a day like this, even in side eddies of the breeze that always
blew through Tijeras Canyon.

From the corner of her vision she noticed the pig eyes of
Sister Clarice glaring at her from the shadow of the sunshade
she wore over her bun of faded-pumpkin hair. The Sister
bobbed her head once, slowly, in and out of its nest of chins,
and twitched her crop against a thigh covered by the pallid
flower-print dress that held her body like a sack of soft potatoes.
Sister Clarice did not much care for Penitential Sister Jillian.
She was too young, too pretty, and much too brown.

Jilly let her gaze slide around and up. And *up*. Up the smooth
stalagmite folds of the robe to the noble Aryan-featured and
thorn-crowned head of He whom the Stewards were conse-
crated to serving: the Christ of the Sandías, the biggest damn
plastic Jesus in Creation, arms outspread in benediction over
the Río Grande Valley and the gates of Hell beyond.

Having transformed woolgathering into apparent piety, Jilly
leaned forward with a sigh. It was just as well she'd gotten
distracted from her line of thought. The stories she had heard
about the Eldest and his nephews . . .

*No. Here. Think about how glad I am I just have to weed
the damn garden instead of digging it. Damn* caliche *is like
cement, and I didn't think you'd find it so far above the river
either . . .*

A commotion, coming up the dirt road. She flicked her gaze aside toward Sister Clarice, ready to snap her eyes back down to the dirt if the Sister happened to be looking her way—she knew from bitter experience what the overseers like Sister Clarice did if you "got forward" with them. But no, Clarice had one slab hand up to augment the green bill of her sunshade, peering toward the gate, where guards were hauling back the great spirals of razor tape with hooks.

It was Buddy—excuse it, the Elder Brother Amos Coffin, nephew of the Supreme Steward himself. He was back a day early with a foraging party that he'd led east along I-40—the Route 66 of ancient legend—into the Sandias proper. Some pretty well-off people had had houses tucked away in the mountain before the latest round of troubles began. Some of them still did.

She hoped they hadn't found one of those. She hated to think of more people winding up in the same mess she was in. If you could believe the gossip in the slave-dorm, she was one of the lucky ones. So far.

"Hallelujah!" Buddy's voice breasted the wind like a bull crossing a mountain stream. He was a boy who liked to make himself heard. "We have found ourselves a genuine miracle of the Lord! Praise *God!*"

"Praise *Jesus.*" the gawkers intoned, and Jilly mumbled something like that too. That was another thing about these people: they were powerfully fond of speaking in exclamation marks.

The door to The Trailer opened, and the Eldest Himself set his blessed foot upon the cheap stamped-metal step, his blessed belly jiggling about the midst of him like a blessed pool toy.

"What have you brought for us, Elder Brother Amos?" he said. He did have a great preacher's voice, rich and resonant and ringing like a bell. Of course he was *shaped* a lot like a bell. Jilly thought that must have something to do with it.

Everyone, slave and overseer and lay brethren alike, seemed to be drifting for the front gate to view Brother Buddy's miracle. *What the heck. I can give my knees a rest, and I'm sick of staring at these stupid weeds.* She felt a flash that maybe in the excitement she could dart through the gate, but she squelched that in a hurry. The gate guards were armed, and they had orders to shoot for the legs, so that anybody who had ideas about shirking the Lord's good work could learn what penitence was *really* all about.

The foraging party laid down a long bundle wrapped in blue plastic. Buddy was strutting back and forth in front of it, his own incipient belly jiggling around inside his white tee-shirt. He had a neck like a boar hog, and most of it was muscle.

"Behold how the Lord has favored us. Look now upon the *miracle* we have brought.'' Rumor said Buddy didn't believe any of that crap, but he knew what side his bread was buttered on, and laid it on thick to please his uncle. He did manage to sound just like a televangelist. Jilly wasn't sure that was much to aspire to.

Then they unrolled the plastic. The crowd gasped.

"Bogus!'' Jilly's mouth exclaimed before she could stop it. "Completely unreal.''

Lots of eyes, all looking her way. Penitentials were to be seen and not heard, unless they were under chastisement.

Sister Clarice was heading her way like a cellulite iceberg. "Girl, I have told you before to watch that tongue of yours—''

But Supreme Steward Coffin had his eyes on her. They burned like hot black lava, and she felt oddly unsettled by them. "Wait,'' he said, holding up a hand. "See what she has to say.''

Now you've done it. On the other hand, she'd never been especially good at keeping it all in, and she'd been keeping a hell of a lot back in the week since she'd been snatched off the farm the Enclave had where the university's south golf course used to be.

She stepped forward and knelt on the edge of the plastic sheet where somebody had dropped a chunk of cinderblock to keep it from whipping up in the wind. The thing on the plastic was unlike anything she'd seen before, outside of some old, old movies. But she knew what it had to be.

"It's a robot,'' she said. "An android. That's a robot shaped like a man.''

"Brother Buddy said it was an angel fall down from Heaven,'' a bearded forager exclaimed. Buddy glared at him.

"Just looks like a big old steel skeleton to me,'' an onlooker said.

"No, see, here in the ribcage by the spine. This housing—

got to be a power source of some sort." She glanced up. "Yep. It's a robot."

"I thought it was a miracle," the forager with the beard complained.

Jilly snorted. "It's not a *miracle*. It's a *kludge*."

"You mean we shagged it all the way back here and it's just a old *robot?*"

"Hush up there, you," Sister Clarice told the forager. "This girl don't know what she's talking about. Lemme just whip a little sense into her now." And the pig eyes gleamed.

Jilly awaited her in a crouch, ready to fight or flee. "Hold on," a young voice said. "Maybe she does know something."

She turned and had some of those mixed feelings she'd always heard about and never really believed in. It was Brother Skip, Hosea Coffin, Buddy's brother. He actually showed the occasional fleeting sign of intelligence. Of course, he did want everybody to call him "Brother Hunk," which was hopelessly optimistic. But he was almost cute in a geeky kind of way, and a definite improvement over his gross brother. Still, he had a way of looking at Jilly and some of the others that didn't make her feel any too secure.

"You, there, Penitential Sister," he said, trying to sound authoritative and squeaking some. "What's your name?"

She stood up straight and tossed her ponytail defiantly over her shoulder. "I'm Jillian Romero."

He nodded at the supine metal man. "What makes you think you know so much about Brother Amos' miracle?"

"I was a cybernetics student at UNM when the Eruption hit. I was still studying as much as I could in the Enclave, when your goons grabbed me."

That brought a warning growl from Sister Clarice. The insides of Jilly's thighs trembled in expectation of the lash, but she realized that by this point she had little left to lose. Sister Clarice was going to take everything out of her hide unless restrained by higher authority no matter what she did now.

"Liberated." Brother Skip flashed what he probably thought was a winning smile at her. "Liberated into the true service of the Lord. But tell us, what's wrong with it?"

"Why the—why would anybody build a robot shaped like a *person?* I mean, the human body is, like, a really mechanically inefficient design, and like we use half our metabolic energy just standing up. You build robots for a *purpose*, you know? Any purpose you can name, there's *lots* more efficient shapes than android.''

''What if the purpose was to make a robot as much like a person as possible?''

She frowned. ''Why would anybody do that?''

''The mundane reasons are not important.'' Supreme Steward Coffin's voice rolled out like an oil slick from a ruptured supertanker. ''It does not matter who made this wondrous man of metal, nor why. The truth is that it is a *divine miracle,* and Providence has guided the hand of the Young Prophet Amos to it to aid Our Lord's work. Praise God, now, sinners! Praise Christ in Living Color!'' He raised his hands toward the colossal statue as the congregation stamped and hollered Amen.

Christ didn't show his true colors till after dark when the bicycle brigade came out, of course. Jilly winced and tried to pull away when Sister Clarice's fingers clamped like red-ant jaws on her earlobe.

''Go ahead,'' the Sister's voice hissed in her ear, ''fight me. Make my day. I'll strip the filthy brown skin off that little fanny of yours, you Mexican slut!''

''Wait!'' Coffin said. ''Peace, now, Sister. Peace.''

Reluctantly Clarice released Jilly's lobe and stepped away. Jilly felt the hate beating off her like heat from a fresh lava flow.

''Providence has directed a new occupation for Penitential Sister Romero. Since she knows so much about our miracle man, she shall have the task of tending to him. Take him to the storage shed, that she may clean the soil from his limbs.''

''Eu,'' Jilly squealed. ''Euuuu, *gross*.'' Her hand snapped back as though it were on an elastic band. The brush she'd been using to free up clumps of black earth and three-needled ponderosa clusters went skittering away on its back across the rudely dressed pine-plank floor like a stunned rat.

''No,'' she said, after a moment sitting in the stultifying afternoon heat of the shed where the dust motes swarmed around her in the slanting sun like gnats. ''No. It can't be. Slavery really is making you crazy, girl.''

She reached her hand, touched the ribcage. The metal felt cool beneath her fingertip, clean. She was unfamiliar with the alloy. She had gotten it clean enough to see that it showed no sign of oxidation, no. tarnish, rust, or patina.

But no, it wasn't her imagination. There was some kind of roughness on the underside of the gleaming sternum arch. She leaned down and squinted.

There were shreds and strings of some kind of blackened, desiccated material inside the ribcage and along the spine. Something like . . . *dried meat.*

She sat up again, sniffed cautiously at the air, as if all of a sudden it was going to reek with putrefaction. No, no scent of decay. But you dried meat to preserve it, she knew that much. If this had been . . . flesh . . . of some kind, the dry mountain air had long since petrified it.

She raised her fingers to her nostrils, sniffed tentatively. Was it her imagination, or was there a tang?

She thought a minute, worrying her lip with even white teeth. Then she pulled out the tail of the nondescript gray work shirt she'd been issued, held it in her teeth. She pulled till a fray in the hem gave, then tore an irregular piece of cloth free.

Ignoring the shivers it sent down her spine, she used her fingernails to scrape a few shreds of the dried organic matter free of the metallic ribcage. She wrapped these in the piece of cloth, folded it into a little bag and tied it with a thread she pulled loose. Then she tucked it deep in a pocket of her grease-stained khaki work pants.

Just doing my duty as a scientist, she told herself. She would have to get the material analyzed at the Enclave. It could be a vital clue as to the origin of this inexplicable artifact, this robot shaped like a man in violation of every principle of efficiency.

That was assuming, of course, she ever made it back to the Enclave to get it analyzed. She pressed her palm over the lump it made in her pocket for a moment, hard.

The dinner bell hung from the end of the prefab barracks that served as chapel and dining hall began to ring. Sunset. Time for the faithful, willing or otherwise, to eat and build up their strength for the nightly devotions.

"Romero?" It was Sister Clarice's voice. Any doubt Jilly had about whether her new responsibility relieved her from having to take part in the service burst with a sickly pop. "Get your butt out here now, girl. There's a power of pedaling for our Lord's Glory to do tonight."

She jumped to her feet and darted out the door.

The scrape of her used-tire sandals had barely died from the gravel outside when two ruby dots appeared on the low wooden ceiling of the shed. For a moment they wandered, independently of each other. Then they snapped into position, three fingers' width apart. In tandem they tracked left, then right, then up and down. Then they vanished.

The gleam died in the eyes set in the sockets of the metal head. The night congealed slowly in the dust that hung in the air.

A plastic wrapper, colors faded to pastel memories by the relentless Southwestern sun, struck the glass-plastic laminate armor windshield of the limo like a bird, slid off to the side and was gone with a trace of nails-on-blackboard screak.

The limousine stopped on the south side of Marquette, facing east. Tay got out of the front passenger's seat, paused to adjust his wraparound shades in the sidestream light of a sun that had already vanished behind the Cubist skyline of Albuquerque's compact downtown. Ignoring the contemptuous stares of a couple of Crips squatting on the curb nearby with long black FN rifles laid across their skinny bare shanks, he walked around to open the rear curbside door for City Councilman Miguel "Mike" Aragon.

Smiling and nodding politely to his bodyguard, Aragon emerged. As he straightened his sports jacket, Dwight, the second of the two bodyguards the treaties permitted him to bring Downtown, stepped out, shutting the door behind him. Like his partner, Dwight was an athletic but caring young man with a moustache and blow-dried hair. Dameron Crowe, Aragon's head of security, thought they were wimps, but Miguel Mike insisted on them. He couldn't relate to the surly author-itarian types Crowe would have stuck him with. Crowe was good at his job but tended to get carried away. Aragon was tolerant. A survivor of Virus-4, Crowe was the size of a ten-year-old and could not walk without crutches. It was not sur-prising that his outlook was sometimes as twisted as his body.

A pair of especially juvenile-looking Crips scrambled up onto the hood. They motioned to the driver to pull away, and he did, slowly, green pennon flapping from the whip antenna on the trunk, the gang members squatting like tan crows in front of the windshield.

Aragon watched them with carefully concealed distaste as the limo turned left on Fourth, to circle back to the underground parking garage beneath Civic Plaza to the east. He understood that the Crips were products of a desire for cultural empow-erment which remained, after all these years of struggle, largely frustrated by the Anglo overculture. But sometimes these kids went too damn far. He was a Chicano himself, after all. And he and the other four meeting here today *were* the City Council.

Someday the Council would find a way to bring the Crips to heel. Until that time, they'd have to swallow their pride and continue to rent the seat of their civic government from the kid gang that actually had hold of it.

"You're late," a Crip sitting on the rail of the T-shaped wheelchair ramp told him. "The *vatos* are here already."

Damn. Vatos meant white people. Aragon always liked to be first to arrive at these weekly sessions; it was important to be punctual, and more than punctual, in order to counteract unfortunate ethnic stereotypes. But now three of the five Coun-cil members were already inside. *Damn.*

A second limo pulled up. This was a superstretch Venezuelan Estrella del Sur *Almirante Cochrane,* black as Hell and armored like a tank beneath its sleek contours, with smoked windows and the engine in back. In front was a pop-up turret designed to take switch-in/switch-out modular weapons trays. At the moment a chain was fastened around the car's long snout like a Christmas ribbon, holding the turret shut. The Crips were very particular about the kind of armament they allowed on their property.

The *Almirante* sported long antennas to either side of the

engine compartment. Brown banners fluttered from them.

"*Aji* madre," Miguel breathed. His timing just couldn't have been worse.

A rangy, dark-skinned man with a shock of straight black hair and an extravagant *bandido* moustache jumped out of the front seat of the limousine. He wore baggy white linen pajama things. His brown feet were bare. By the way the Crip on the railing glowered at him and spat, Aragon gathered that the man was a Mexican national. Crips didn't have much use for birth-Mexicans. He wasn't good at telling things like that himself.

The Mexican opened the rear door. A barrel-chested man got out, grunting under the weight of his astonishing belly. Aragon breathed a sigh of relief. *At least he's not wearing his bandit suit tonight*. The Council member for the heavily Latino South Valley loved to play to all the very stereotypes that went straight up Miguel "Mike" Aragon's back.

Tom González stood up, straightened his white tropical suit around his shaved-bear frame. He noticed Aragon. "Ah, Miguelito. *Mikey*. So good to see you." And he waddled up and gave Miguel an *abrazo* that almost dislocated his spine.

As his own limo pulled away González walked out halfway toward the police and sheriff building across the street. Putting hands on hips beneath the tails of his coat, he craned off toward the mountains to the east.

"Should be about time," he said, half to himself. With a chest like that, he could talk to himself and people would hear him in Aragon's district clear across the river. "Well, come on, *coño*, hurry it up. We ain't got all night."

Aragon frowned at him. González did an odd bird dance, coming down flatfoot on both feet, stretching up and left, coming back flatfoot again, stretching right.

A glow shone forth from the foothills north of Tijeras Canyon. González whooped and jumped, stabbing both fists in the air. "Green! I told you it would be green! *¡Hijo la!*"

Aragon came out into the middle of the street to see what on Earth he was raving about. That stupid Christ of the Sandias had come on.

"What's going on?" Aragon asked.

"The *Cristo*. He came on green." He turned to his body-guard, who was pouting beneath his moustache. "Pay up, *carnal*."

"It's pink."

"So what? It's white now. He came on green. You ain't no betting man, are you, Miguelito?"

He squeezed his fellow Councilor's cheek. "Come on, *cuate,* we got business to do. Or you gonna stand out here in the street all night staring at that dumb statue?"

Blinking a little in the glare of track lights that pinned those who dared address the City Council to the lectern like a barrage of laser beams, Colonel George Donelson, USAF, commanding officer, 223rd Special Security Group, raised his head—hair close-cropped and sandy, the harsh hot light playing on the bald spot like the moon on the chromed bumper of a '57 Chevy at a late Twentieth Century drive-in outside Jal—from his notes to face the five Councilors on their dais.

"It has been twenty-three months since the series of volcanic eruptions began which have been responsible for the ever-increasing disorder in the Albuquerque area." He paused for effect. "I don't think any of us can be proud of our record since that time." He thought his voice was firm and manly, crisp with the ring of command. Actually it was kind of reedy.

The Chicano Councilor—the fatter one, with the white suit and ridiculous moustache—stubbed his cigar in the ashtray before him, to the visible relief of his fellow members.

"If you mean the disgraceful failure of the so-called Federal government to provide financial relief for the unfortunate victims of all these natural disasters, I couldn't agree more, Colonel. With only a little help and encouragement, the independent township of González could be a thriving reality, instead of a captive community subject to all the whims of racist and retrograde Gringo Albuquerque."

Scattered applause broke out from behind Donelson. Scattered was generally the only way applause came in the Council chambers. The Crips let anybody who wanted to come in to attend Council meetings—the only limitation was on the number of armed goons the Councilors could bring—but few bothered. Usually the only audience consisted of hired claques the Council members brought with them, representatives from Albuquerque's small and servile media, and the inexplicable few petitioners who thought it was worthwhile to address a governing body with absolutely no *de facto* power.

And tonight, of course, Colonel Donelson.

"Oh, *Thomas*," Councilwoman Brand said. She turned aside her head that squeezed like a bubble out of the high lace collar clamped on her throat. Her tightly coiffed hair was an unearthly yellow in the blazing light. Before going into politics she had been a highly successful author of children's books. She represented—which was to say, *ran*—the southeastern section of town, which lay nearest Kirtland Base. As base security officer and second-in-command, Donelson had all too frequent occasion to talk to her. She had probably not been unattractive at one point, but she was trying to fight the encroachments of middle age by hanging on to girlhood, a strategy you didn't have to be a trained strategic thinker like Donelson to know wouldn't work. "Perhaps we *should* just let you go your own way."

"Now, Barbara," Ross Maynet said from her left, "you surely can't mean that. You yourself are constantly stressing the values of *community*." He was a small, sleek, blinking blond man in a beige suit. He had been Albuquerque's Shoe King as well as City Councilor when the Eruption hit.

"I'm compelled to agree with my colleague from the Near Heights," said Dino DiStefano. He had been a successful attorney before things blew up. He was a tall man in his early fifties, what your civilians called *distinguished,* fit-looking in a conservative blue pinstripe, with tightly waved black hair gone striking silver at the temples. "Seeking a strong center is our foremost mission in these troubled times. Don't you agree, Councilor Aragon?"

The member in the middle jerked, as if he'd been dozing off. He was the youngest of the group, and despite the fact he was carrying less weight than González, offended the fitness-minded Donelson the most. He was *sloppy*. He was also something of a wimp.

Just let me get you out on the parade ground for some serious PT, buddy, Donelson thought. *I'd burn that lard off in a hell of a hurry.*

"Well, uh, naturally. Naturally, government—our role *as* government is, ah, to assure that we have the power to serve the public. But Mr. González does have a point, I must remind the Council. His district, the South Valley, has been treated

like an unwanted appendage of Albuquerque for many years.
On the other hand—''

Wimp, Donelson thought. But Aragon had briefly been chair-
man of the State Film Commission and worked for the public
defender's office before getting elected to the Council. What
could you expect?

The colonel cleared his throat into the mike. Everyone
jumped. Anyone who'd lived in Albuquerque over the last
couple of years was *very* conscious of rumbling sounds.

"If we might return to the subject—gentlemen, Ms. Brand—
I feel there is no substantial disagreement here. We all agree
on the need for restoring order and discipline to everyday life.
The Federal government, through its lawful representatives—
meaning, in the current disorganized state of affairs, the military contingent at Kirtland Base—stands ready to provide assistance to a strong, unified city government.''

He paused, freckled hands gripping the lectern, giving a
steely-eyed glare to each Councilor in turn.

"The fact is, we find no such government. We find, instead,
a city divided into five major armed and mutually hostile camps,
plus a veritable horde of lesser factions. We find a city council
which seems to comprise nothing more than a social club for
the heads of the largest fiefdoms. We find a city government
which has to rent its administrative and even its police and jail
facilities from a gang of street toughs.''

That brought a growl from the Crips keeping an eye on the
proceedings from the rear. He smiled thinly beneath his moustache. *Let them try something. Let them.* His Blue Berets were
itching for the chance to teach these bastards a lesson or two.

The Councilors all started talking at once, except González,
who smirked, slouched lower in his chair on the right flank,
and lit another cigar. Aragon tried to restore order, making
gestures with his hand as if he were trying to pat out a burning
napkin. He sweated profusely.

"A F-f-federal government worthy of the *name,*" Maynet
said, finally making himself heard by virtue of shrillness,
"would not have to ask!''

"Once again I have to agree with my good friend Ross,
despite our doctrinal differences," DiStefano said. "It seems
incumbent on the United States to determine whom it recog-
nizes as the legitimate government of Albuquerque. Of all of

New Mexico, come to that, since administration of the state as a whole has been sadly in abeyance since the destruction of Santa Fe.''

Donelson pursed his mouth. ''There's turmoil all across the country. There have been budget cutbacks—''

''Thank you so much for sharing your valuable time with us, Colonel,'' Barbara Brand said. ''We really can't impose on you any more.''

''But—''

''Perhaps when you have concrete proposals as to what the Federal government plans to do to assist us in reestablishing legitimate authority, you might again grace us with your presence,'' DiStefano said.

''Or when you get the Feds to cough up some aid,'' González said, puffing like a fumarole.

Donelson stood to attention, glared at them, then turned and marched stiffly from the lectern.

Amateurs, he thought, and then the ultimate insult: *civilians.*

You'll be laughing out the other side of your mouths in short order, you slugs. Just as soon as Los Alamos comes through.

He couldn't help himself. He had to laugh out loud.

Miguel ''Mike'' Aragon watched the colonel's shiny head recede down the aisle and wondered just what the man found so funny. He was in here every couple of months, urging the Council to submit to martial law. General Whiteman, the base commander, was a lovely man, sensitive, a fine cellist. But he had a career military man's perspective, and that just wasn't appropriate for a city in torment. You couldn't solve the problems of poverty and injustice that were really responsible for the crisis by barking orders at them.

Not that Paul—General Whiteman—would handle things that way. But his second-in-command was another story. He was always polite enough, but Miguel Mike thought he had a kind of crazy gleam in those pale blue eyes.

''W-what's next on the agenda, Mike?'' Maynet asked.

Aragon looked down at the printout in front of him. His heart sank.

As if on cue the rear door of the chambers burst open and a tall, lanky Latino marched in at the head of a pack of Crips, male and female. He wore rope sandals, loose tropical-weight white trousers, a shirt printed with gaudy red flowers. A matching bandanna was wound about his clean-shaven head. A floppy straw hat with a band that also matched topped off the outfit. His near-skeletal features were made up with an alarming ochre base that he claimed emphasized his natural color; his eyes were lined, lashes lengthened, lips painted Dracula red. He looked like a Jersey City matron hitting the beach in Puerto Rico after a bout with chemotherapy. What he was was head of the Crips.

Aragon sighed. His stomach started to burn. He ate only healthy foods. It seemed unfair, to subsist on a diet of tofu and mung sprouts and still get heartburn. Maybe Maynet had some Tums on him.

"Next on the agenda," he read, "is Mr. Skin."

The street-gang contingent, heavily armed and looking like the Khmer Rouge blowing into Phnom Penh for the weekend, took their seats in the front few rows, rousting out the professional applauders. The Crip boss posed for a heartbeat with an elbow on the lectern and his fingertips resting on a yellow cheek. The irises of his eyes were silver-pale, almost white.

"*Do* excuse me for a moment," he said with a hint of a lisp. He fished in the breast pocket of his Hawaiian shirt. "You insist on keeping the lights so *blindingly* bright."

He settled a pair of batwing sunglasses on the bridge of his nose. Rhinestones fired glints of dazzle at the Council like machinegun bullets.

"There. That's ever so much better."

"To what do we owe the pleasure, Mr. Skin?" DiStefano asked, voice honey smooth with irony.

Plucked eyebrows rose into view from behind the shades. "What? You don't know? Well, I suppose that shouldn't surprise us for a moment, should it, boys and girls?"

He turned to his followers, who waved tattooed arms and cheered.

"I assume you're speaking of that unfortunate young woman," Aragon said hastily.

"Precisely. Early this morning we found the body of a woman hanging from a chain in an abandoned warehouse on Second Street. She was nude and had apparently been tortured and raped before being killed. This is the third slasher-style slaying in Albuquerque in the last four months. It's the first to take place on Crip turf.

"Frankly, it's unacceptable for you to permit your problems to spill into our territory. We are trying to attract outside investment in order to revitalize the downtown area, and something like this simply *doesn't help*."

"We understand you saw fit to interfere with our investigators, Mr. Skin," Maynet said, speaking very precisely. "Since you bring the point up, it seems ironic that you should claim to be independent of our jurisdiction, and yet when you fall victim to the same senseless street crime that's sweeping America, you cry to us for help."

"For *help?* Mr. Maynet, when I arrived on the scene this morning I found one of your homicide detectives tossing the victim's left shoe—an imitation cloisonné pattern, silver on blue, quite fetching in a naïve way—in his hand as if it were a Dunkin Donut. And without an evidence tech anywhere in sight. Tell me, Mr. Maynet, where did your police learn their investigative technique? Saturday morning cartoons?

"And that poor girl—such a shame. She probably had been quite lovely. Unfortunately, she was there for at least a day before we discovered her. I fear I shall never get the smell out of my outfit, and it's a Sans Souci original from Ouagadougou."

" 'Girl?' " Brand sniffed. "Our information indicates she was in her middle thirties. That's hardly a *girl*, Mr. Skin."

"We took possession of the other shoe and certain other effects before your police could mingle more of their fingerprints and bodily fluids with the murderer's. They are being analyzed at the University Enclave at Crip expense."

"The Enclave," Maynet sniffed. That was another sore spot for the Council. "If those ivory t-tower—"

The council chamber shook.

The lights dimmed. "*Eruption!*" Aragon heard somebody scream. He realized it was him.

The lights came up again. Through a break between panels of the cloth hung like a curtain on the front of the table the Council sat behind, Aragon saw Mr. Skin standing with his arms crossed on the lectern, smirking at them and shaking his head as a snowstorm of insulation and ceiling-panel dust fluttered on his hat and shoulders.

"My, my, my," the Crip chieftain said as the Councilors picked themselves up from under the table. "Afraid of a little bitty volcano, are we? If you hadn't been in such a hurry to flee to the mountains and save your precious skins when the first Eruption hit, you might not have found us in charge here when you came creeping back."

"Your occupation of the Downtown area is manifestly illegal," DiStefano said, standing to dust off the knees of his trousers. "Not to mention the extortion you wring from us for letting us use our own facilities."

Mr. Skin spread his hands and smiled. "Why, Mr. DiStefano, all you have to do is unite against us. We are cunning fighters, and brave—" He turned and shook a fist. The Crips clapped and wolf-called. "—But we are supreme realists. We know full well that should even two of you manage to lay aside your differences long enough to cooperate to drive us out, we should be swept aside like the paper streamers and soda cups after a fiesta."

The smile widened. His teeth were long and yellow and jumbled, like bowling pins stuck head-down in his shrunken gums.

"Yet somehow that never happens."

Miguel "Mike" Aragon moistened his lips and darted glances left and right at his fellow Councilors. They sat as if turned into mannequins, staring straight ahead.

"Listen to me, O powerful City Council: find the killer. Let your people strangle each other in their little frame-stucco houses, let your followers bushwhack one another in your border disputes. But don't let your serial killers stray into our Downtown. We don't want your problems here."

He walked from the podium to applause like a full-auto ambush, shaking clasped hands over his head. Cheering and waving their weapons, his followers trooped after him, out the door and out of the chamber.

"Ahh," Aragon said, self-conscious about breaking the silence, "according to police reports, the murdered woman worked at the Treasure Box north of town."

Brand's breath hissed in over small sharp teeth. "*That* place."

"Like the first two," DiStefano said. "What more evidence

do we need? That place is a bleeding ulcer on our city. It's time we took steps.''

"That kind of exploitation of women is what causes tragedies such as this," Brand said, folding her hands.

Maynet had been fighting to get a word out, and finally succeeded: "Im-m-m-morality! It's the b-breakup of the family, a decline of Judeo-Christian morals. All these drugs and p-pornography. It's the terrible cost of liberty in this country."

"Certainly, the rights junkies have much to answer for," DiStefano intoned.

"We can only expect turmoil when the supposed rights of individuals interfere with the rights of the community," Brand said.

"The Treasure Box *is* a good example of what happens when free enterprise runs unchecked," Miguel Aragon said. He liked to make sure he stayed with the consensus. *The nail that stands out must be hammered down*—sometimes that seemed harsh, but it was the only way to run a truly caring society.

DiStefano nodded gravely. "It's decided. We need to take decisive action to bring these people into line. We should do something about the Enclave, too. Colonel Donelson was right in his own militaristic way: until we can impose our authority more effectively on the dissidents, things like this will happen."

Another tremor hit. The Council stood its ground this time.

"*Cabrones*," Tom González said, scratching a stick match alight with a cracked and dirty thumbnail. "Why don't we just concentrate on catching this fucker?"

They all looked at him as if he were crazy.

3

A fly lit on the bridge of Jilly's nose, a big startling black blur close up by her right eye. She recoiled and batted at it. It floated away, gliding on the current of air driven by her slapping hand, then began to turn lazy droning figure-eights around her head, contemptuous of her ability to connect.

From the packed-earth yard outside came the stomping and bull-roar shouts of Brother Buddy drilling the Mount Zion Fortress of Faith defense forces. It was the kind of afternoon that really weighed down your eyelids. It promised to be hotter than the last one.

Just when I think I'm getting used to the smell around here, she thought, *the damn flies remind me.* She wrinkled her nose, scratched the spot where the fly had landed. She was getting pretty ripe too, come to think of it. It drove her crazy. She'd always been kind of a bug on cleanliness, and the odor of her own unwashed body was a reproach to her. But showers were a privilege a Penitential had to earn—and trying too hard to earn one got you suspected of being too much in thrall to the Prince of This World.

That was what the Eldest Brother and Revelatory Prophet called Satan, whom he regarded as a personal antagonist and immediate cause of anything that went wrong. In fact, Reverend Coffin seemed pretty strongly convinced that Old Nick Himself prowled the perimeter of the hilltop community on a regular basis. Dorm gossip said your more alert sentries reported finding cloven hoofprints just outside the wire from time to time, although demonic influences managed to wipe them out before anybody else got a chance to look at them. Brother Zephaniah knew they'd *been* there, though.

Brother Zephaniah was long overdue for a head upgrade, in Jilly's humble opinion.

A squeak of gravel under bootsoles galvanized her. She grabbed the wood chisel they'd issued her to get the stringy dried stuff off their new miracle and began to scrape away. The idea of using the right tool for the job was another idea that went right over these people's pointy heads.

"On with the buff and wax, Max," she told the robot. *Metal Max* was the name she'd given him, in her head. She was used to living much of her life in her head. It had gotten her through childhood, and it was turning out to be a real survival skill now. Which was fortunate, because as she saw it she didn't *have* many survival skills.

From the force and cadence of the approaching footsteps she knew they were male, and Buddy was still hollering at the Lord's Avenging Angels like Sergeant Dirk Dagger, Strike Force, and when the Big Man himself walked the very earth trembled, so she wasn't surprised when a skinny adolescent shadow fell across the outstretched skeletal legs of the robot.

She looked up, then dropped her eyes in what a few brisk cracks on the fanny, courtesy of Sister Clarice, had taught her was appropriate modesty. "The Prophet Hosea blesses me with his radiance," she murmured. *Jee-zus*, she thought.

He blinked and slid his cowboy boots around on the plank for a second, then smiled. "You can call me 'Hunk,'" he said.

Only if I want to get the giggles real bad and swallow my tongue. "As the Prophet commands," she said. "With the Prophet's permission, I shall return to the task the Senior Steward has set me." *Give me a break! Do you believe this crap?*

"I've been reading books on administration all morning," he announced. "When the scales of Satan drop from the eyes of the multitudes and they start flocking to Salvation, I'm going to have my hands pretty full helping run things. And that's going to happen any day now."

Jilly desperately wanted to make a cylinder of thumb and fingers and do jack-off gestures in the dusty air.

"How's the work going, Penitential Sister?"

I should do *something,* she thought. *But what? Am I going to hold this stupid chisel to his neck and take him hostage? Should I maybe threaten him with my block-handle wire brush?*

She hated herself for being so useless. She wished she had learned some kind of self-defense skills as a girl—savate, karate, anything. The Japanese must have some kind of martial art devoted to fighting with common hand tools—they were a methodical people, and certainly they had every *other* kind of martial art imaginable. But her parents would never have permitted it, and she was always too much of a little goody-goody to do anything like take lessons behind their backs. They had been horrified enough when she announced she wanted to be a cyberneticist; they had their hearts set on their little girl being a human resource engineer for the government, just like they were. That had been the highwater mark in rebellion for her life.

"It, uh, it goes well, Prophet." *Jeez, keep awake, girl. You piss this one off, there's no telling what'll happen.* It occurred to her there was no telling what would happen as it was, but she saw no point in stirring things up.

He seemed to have an interest in technology, or at least technobabble. "As you see, the alloy from which the robot is made is very hard. No matter how hard I dig at it with this chisel, it doesn't leave so much as a scratch."

"That's very interesting. But I thought I told you to call me—" He stopped and sighed and hunkered down across the robot from her.

"Oh, well. Call me Skip, or Hosea, or whatever. I'm not very good at this kind of thing."

What *kind of thing?* she wondered with alarm. Nothing seemed the safest thing to say, so she said it.

"What else are you finding out about Brother Buddy's miracle?" he asked.

"Not a whole lot yet, Proph—Skip. If a miserable slave might be permitted to ask a question—" *Eu, gag.* "—just where did your Blessed Brother find this thing?"

"Some kind of plane crash, up near the old ranger station on Cedro Peak. Why?"

She nodded. "That explains something. See the left forearm? Instead of just imitating normal human bones like the other arm, it's built in kind of a reinforced armature to hold this big tube."

"And what's the tube for?"

It looks like a carbon lasing and boosting chamber, she thought, but she wasn't ready to tell them that. "I'm not sure. But look at this thing here."

"The round thing? Like a bowl, or maybe a socket or something?"

"Bingo. It seems to be a housing that something fitted into. And that something seems to have gotten itself torn out with a hell—heck of a lot of force. See? It's the same alloy as the rest of this thing, and it's *scratched.*"

Skip whistled.

"Yeah. And look at this—" She started to rattle on about how marvelously the joints were machined, but he wasn't listening.

"You don't like me, do you?" he blurted in mid-exposition.

Uh-oh. Danger, Will Robinson, danger. She dropped her eyes. "The Prophet Hosea lights my life with his radiance—"

"Oh, screw that. *Look* at me."

He grabbed her chin and raised her head. Her cheeks tightened, but she kept herself from pulling away.

Abruptly he snatched his hand back, as if her cheeks were actually as hot as they felt. "I'm sorry. Look. I—I know you don't like being a Penitential. I don't like it much myself."

What? Being a Penitential? Articulacy was not the boy's strong point.

"We have to have Penitentials, until the Radiant Christ burns the blinders off the eyes of a few more sinners and they step forward to help with the Work. He can't shine His light in Living Color if we don't have people to pedal the bikes that give Him power. So we have to *have* more people in order to *save* more people, and that's why we sometimes have to round up poor sinners to be Penitentials, so that someday nobody will have to *be* a Penitential anymore. Do you see? It's like—like—''

It's kind of like a feedback loop, Jilly thought, but she didn't feel like letting him off the hook.

He shook his head as if trying to shake off the sentence he didn't know how to finish like one of the omnipresent flies. ''Anyway. I put in a good word for you with the Steward. You don't have to bicycle any more.''

She looked at him in surprise. She did hate to ride the frapping bikes, even though you had to figure it was aerobic. ''I thank the Prophet Hosea,'' she said, remembering to lower her eyes again.

''Hey, it's nothing—Jillian. May I call you Jillian?''

''A Prophet of the Lord may call me anything he chooses.''

''Look, I don't want to be a Prophet to you. I want to be your friend.''

She worked at the dried tissue-like stuff. It really was pretty tenacious. Outside the troops were doing hand-to-hand combat drill.

''I'm trying to work it so you won't have to be a Penitential anymore.''

She struggled not to look at him.

''The Highest Prophet said he'd think about it. But you have to get us some results, Jillian. Is there anything—you have any idea how to make him work? The robot, I mean. Is there any sign he might still run?''

Jilly sat on her heels. The tip of her tongue stuck out between lips that felt as dry as the Jornada del Muerte.

There *was* something. But it was totally screwy. Every once in a while, she had the oddest feeling of *presence* when she was around Metal Max.

What that probably meant was that some of her chips were starting to work loose, what with the strain of being *property* to a bunch of religious ding-dongs. Even if there was something to it, though, she wasn't about to mention it to Brother Hunk here. These people were liable to get the notion she'd given their miracle man the evil spirits or something and burn her for a witch.

''Nothing, Skip,'' she said. She caught herself about to smile at him, then thought *what the heck* and did smile. "I'll let you know if I learn anything concrete."

"Thanks. It could be important. For the Lord's work, and also for you."

He stood up. "Well, I better get back and hit the books. A Great Awakening's coming, and time waits for no man."

In the doorway he stopped and turned back. The fierce sun caught the side of his face and turned his dirty-blond hair to gold.

"I just want you to like me," he said and practically ran out the door.

For a long hot-afternoon moment Jilly stared after him. Then, shaking her head, she bent to her work.

You know, he's almost sweet. In a total geek kind of way.

She could have told him a lot more—as it was she was afraid she might have told him too much, pointing out the maybe-laser tube in Max's left arm. Because between the artificial bones of the robot's *right* forearm was another curious device. It was a black case of what looked like polyceram, polymerized ceramic, perhaps seven inches long and two inches wide at the upper end, tapering slightly to match the contour of the arm.

The palm of the right hand had a hole in it. If you bent the hand back so Max seemed to be making a "stop" gesture, the hole lined up with a polyceram-lined channel through the wrist and aligned perfectly with a hole in the front of the black case.

It didn't correspond to anything in Jilly's experience. But she was a hardware hacker, by training and inclination, and she had a strong intuition for how form matched function.

She thought she knew what the mystery case was. She *thought* it was a gun.

She *knew* one thing: If her new boyfriend Max was some kind of robot killing machine, she would damn sure keep the Plastic Jesus Freaks from being able to put him to use for their sicko crusade. No matter what it cost her. Even if it meant spending the rest of her life pumping away on a lousy Exer-cycle. Even if . . .

No. She'd heard enough dormitory gossip to have too good an idea of just what the downside could be, if they thought she was holding out on them. She would pay that price, too, for her friends back at the Enclave, the only family the Big Valley Barbecue had left her. But she would not think about it.

"Well, Max," she said, whistling past the grave. "Looks like it's just you and me against the world, huh, kid?"

For a fleeting splinter of an instant she *felt* it, that intangible pressure against the skin, as if there were someone else in the room with her. She stared at the robot, hair raising at her nape beneath the bun into which she had wound her heavy black ponytail. She waited for it to move, half expectant, half fearful.

Nothing. She picked up her wire brush and, whistling a Brazilian pop tune she'd heard on Mohammed's Radio, she bent back to work.

4

In his faded yellow Sears bathrobe and his blue plastic flipflop sandals, the Supreme Steward, Eldest Brother, Revelatory Prophet, and Senior Prophet of the Church of Christ in Living Color, Protector and Patriarch of the Mount Zion Fortress of Faith, and Master Illuminator of the Way of Christ on Earth Zephaniah Coffin stood outside his trailer and watched the light drain from the western sky.

He loved this time of day best of all. He hardly ever slept, so he got to see plenty of dawns, but in God's truth they weren't much; with the bulk of the mountains pushing right up against them from the east, the sky was pretty well lit by the time you made the day's first acquaintance with the sun.

Besides, there was nothing to compare with a spring evening like this. The air was cool and sweet, but you could still smell the heat the rocks had spent the whole day gathering, like the smell of warm denim. And the lights of Albuquerque—devil's den though it undoubtedly was—all spread out, symbolically at his feet, like fistfuls of jewels strewn on a jeweler's black velvet rug.

It was going . . . there; *gone,* the last of day, except for a teensy thin pale turquoise strip right along the horizon, and a couple gauzy patches of red oozing up out of the two main calderas, over across the river—nothing much exciting going on over there tonight, praise the Lord, though eruptions could be a spectacular sight from way up here. They were of the devil, though.

And now it was time. He caught a breath, let a bit of it out and held it, as if he were squeezing a trigger. And the whip-cracks came, and the first shrill of whistles, and then, slow and low at first, droning, then rising to crescendo like a mighty cicada chorus, came the whir of half a hundred bicycles, being pedaled for all they were worth.

And Christ's glory exploded from His image like the fireball of a hydrogen bomb. Yellow for starters tonight.

"Ahhhh." The air gusted out of Coffin in a long, humid, happy exhalation. For him this was always the best moment. Better even than ejaculation, and the Supreme Steward was a man who liked to come.

He turned and put his foot on the step. There was still the Lord's work to attend to before he could ease his spirit for the night.

From time immemorial there have been Coffins, and there always will be Coffins. For the most part they are men of the same cloth: tall men, burned gaunt by the hot fires of the Lord that rage behind their pale eyes. Men with long-drawn faces and dome foreheads who hate as good Christians ought. Men who never shrink from touching the torch to faggots piled under cringing feet.

Zephaniah Coffin, Supreme Steward and Eldest Brother of the Church of Christ in Living Color, departed somewhat from the classic Coffin somatotype, but only physically. He was tall, as befit a Coffin, and his forehead was a high and noble bluff—Coffin men begin to thin early, but miraculously never go bald. But below the shoulders the classic lean Coffin lines went sadly astray. He was, to be blunt, pear-shaped.

The trailer's cluttered insides were yellow-lit, flickering and dim. Forage had been good of late, and the Mt. Zion teams had turned up plenty of salvage to trade for kerosene or alcohol to burn in the lamps—much as the Eldest hated to dirty his hands with trade, preferring to accept free-will donations from the faithful or wring tribute by God-granted strength from the limbs of Satan who had not eyes to see, sometimes he simply had to. It was one of the trials set for the pure in heart.

Still, though the tanks the Supreme Steward had laid away underground before the first Eruption brimmed with fuel, he kept his lamps turned low. He was frugal. Also he liked the half-lit effect when granting audiences to the flocks. It lent the proper aura of gravity and mystery.

"So, sons of my lamented sister," he said to his two nephews, "what would you have of me?"

Buddy looked at Skip. Skip looked at the sharkskin tips of his cowboy boots.

"Hosea's been sniffing around that new girl. That little Meskin Penitential one."

Coffin Senior sighed heavily, made his heavy way between the piles of papers, mainly tracts, mainly his, that rose in waist-high piles from tables and from the thin floral-print carpet. He bent ponderously to pick up a pie pan with a chunk of crust drying in it from the accustomed spot he left cleared of tracts on his favorite faded, bow-legged, ancient sofa. Sister Louise was getting mighty slovenly about policing up the remnants of the pies that were the Steward's favored food. He might have to order her a dozen or so strokes of contrition, across her well-padded but nicely shaped buttocks. Or maybe it would make a greater impression *not* to—the Lord's Chief Shepherd knew his flocks well, and nothing got Sister Louise quite as warm and runny as a few fresh stripes on her cheeks.

He sat and regarded his nephews.

"I was just trying to see how her work was coming," Skip said defensively. "If we're going to command an empire of the Faithful, we have to know how to keep an eye on things."

"Horse puckey," Buddy said. "He just wants to diddle her, Uncle."

Coffin's tongue worked around the inside of his teeth, scouting for any overlooked remains of dinner.

"My sister, may her eternal disposition weigh lightly upon her, was a wild woman. A good woman at heart, but unable to look away when Satan sported his wiles. You are both the products of sin, to be frank. Keeping you free of the same claws that drew your poor mother down to probable perdition is a full-time job.''

He cocked his head. ''Mind, I hear him now. My Adversary. He's out there a-prowlin' by the wire, snuffling and whuffling, his cloven hooves crunching in the sand.''

He picked up one of the fake Hummel figurines that gave the tracts and pie crust a run for horizontal space in the trailer. The Revelatory Prophet liked to run his fingers over them, liked their cool hard smoothness, their rose-pink cheeks.

''But, Uncle,'' Skip whined, ''all I wanted was to see what she found out. I'm real interested in robots. You know that.''

Buddy started to make a jack-off gesture with his right hand, thought better of it in time.

''You are interested in her *tits*, Hosea,'' Coffin Senior said severely. ''They are like unto rosebuds, swelling, about to blossom forth in their full glory. You are too much taken with things of this world, boy. It's another sign of the taint in you. But still, if this robot can be put to the Lord's work, it is certainly true we'd be spitting in the eye of Providence if we didn't put it to use. What, exactly, has that little girl learned to make the robot do?''

Skip chewed his lower lip and studied his boots some more. ''Uh. Nothing, Uncle. Not yet—but these scientific things take time. You can't rush them.''

Coffin transferred his attention to his other nephew, who had his thick arms crossed over his chest and was smirking. ''Tell me again, Amos, where you found your miracle man?''

''Up in a side canyon near Cedro Peak, off south 14. Plane wreck of some kind.''

''You didn't find any other equipment? No papers or manuals or disks? Nothing that might be instructions?''

''No, sir. All we found was the nose of this aircraft with the robot pinned under it. We reckoned it must of busted itself all to pieces on the peaks coming in. Or maybe it even blew up in midair.'' He shrugged. ''Looked like it'd been there a year, maybe two.'' It looked that way to one of his forage party, he meant. Buddy had been leading patrols through these mountains since before Eruption, and still had all the woods lore of a fire hydrant.

Zephaniah Coffin pursed his lips into a blossom of pink and gray gristle. ''I shall think about it. Leave me now.''

The boys started out the door. "Amos? Attend me a moment longer, if you please."

Amos halted inside the door. Skip cast a despairing glance back at his uncle and went out into the night, letting the warped-aluminum screen door bang against the frame.

"He's too young, yet," Zephaniah Coffin said. "He wants seasoning."

Buddy licked his lips. "Not me though, Uncle. Huh?" Real quick on the uptake, this boy.

The Eldest shook his head. "You too are weak. But you are not *as* weak. You keep one thing in mind, boy—no vessel is pure enough for the likes of you until it has been purified by me. The Devil's out there now, waiting his chance to claim you for his own, the way he claimed your mother. You mind that, boy."

Buddy stuck out his lower lip. "Yes, Uncle."

"I think we've given that little girl more than enough chance to produce results with her godless science. My, what a firm, round little rump she has." Coffin set down the figurine. "Sister Clarice says the other Penitentials are getting antsy about her getting out of pedaling for glory and other such chores, and we don't want to be responsible for increasing their burden of the sin of envy, do we?

"Tomorrow Penitential Romero can finish getting your Miracle Man all polished up. Maybe we can put him on display as a paying attraction for the sinners. I've long thought there should be a way to tap the potential of the tourist industry to do the Lord's good work. Pass the word to Sister Clarice that she's to go back to regular Penitential duties."

Buddy nodded, started out the door. "Bide a moment," his uncle said. "As I think about it, maybe you better tell Sister Clarice to get her all fixed up nice once she finishes cleaning the robot. I feel she's being called to higher service."

Buddy's eyes gleamed.

"There should be a petitioner waiting outside. Send her in when you go, boy."

Buddy left. A moment later Coffin heard the creak of the door-latch and Sister Joleen entered with a step as tentative as a fawn in a morning meadow.

"Eldest Brother," she said, keeping her eyes demurely downcast. A strand of lank red hair fell in her eyes and she brushed it away with a quick gesture, almost furtive. "I have come before you with a humble petition."

He filled his eyes with her. She was young and fair of form, if perhaps a trifle slatternly. The Supreme Steward didn't mind. He knew when to overlook minor details in the furtherance of God's great plan.

"You may speak, child."

"Senior Prophet, it has been three months since I have lain with my husband. He's borne it well, but lately he's gotten, well, kind of cranky. And to tell you the truth, I—"

She peeked at him quickly between her bangs, looked at the floor again. "I've been getting a little bit of an itch myself."

"Child, you make me proud," he rumbled deep in his chest, "the way you've withstood the blandishments of the Devil for so long. After such a struggle, it seems a shame to give in."

He let his chin sink in thought. Sister Joleen licked her lips. She seemed to quiver as she stood there by the door, watching him.

"I have it," the Prophet said at last. "Rather than let all your strugglin' and forbearance go for naught, you shall slake the fires of your sinful lust in the waters of my holiness. And maybe—yes. I think we should get Sister Alicia in to help us with this. This is my judgment."

She gave a small, sharp gasp. She raised her blue eyes to his and smiled.

It was what she'd hoped he'd say.

5

"No!" Jilly screamed. Her words bounced around among the crowded cots and roof trusses of the otherwise deserted slave dorm. "No, I don't believe you."

Sister Clarice gripped her biceps with hands like upholstered C-clamps. "It's Lord's truth, girl. You're to get Brother Buddy's Miracle Man all shined up nice tomorrow, and then you're back with the other Penitentials."

It should have been no surprise. The Supreme Steward wanted results. Also, these people *owned* Jilly, and they were crazy. Nothing they did should have surprised her.

But Jillian Romero was nineteen years old. Just when she thought she was going to get out of adolescence alive, just when she'd finally begun to learn to deal with the loss of her family and her carefully-planned future in the volcanic fires of Eruption, strange hands had laid hold of her and dragged her into this bad hallucinogenic trip.

And here was this hateful woman, her big bloated face gloating down on her like a full moon over a misshapen mountain, telling her she was going back to the drudgery and constant anxiety of a common slave. Inside her something just snapped.

Despite the woman's brutish strength, Jilly pulled free and started to run. Where, she didn't know.

Sister Clarice was built like a nose tackle gone to seed, but she was snake-quick. She caught Jilly by the ponytail and reined her up sharply.

Jilly wheeled and slapped her in the face.

For a moment Sister Clarice stood there. Then she reared back, nostrils flaring and eyes rolling like a fighting bull facing the *banderilleros*. She slammed Jilly to the raw board floor with an openhand slap that set lights flashing and the whole room spinning.

Through the high singing in her head Jilly became aware of a still shriller sound, rhythmic and insistent. After an indeterminate moment—there seemed to be something wrong with her time sense—she comprehended that Sister Clarice had her rape whistle out and was blowing on it for all she was worth, cheeks puffing and eyes bulging. She must have had sound veins, because if she'd had any aneurysms she'd be blowing them out for sure.

The room filled up with eyes. It was shift-change time on the Christcycles—Eldest Brother Coffin knew his slaves had to rest sometime. And here came guards from the duty shack, clutching shotguns and rifles, wild-eyed with eagerness to shoot somebody, *anybody,* for the Prince of Peace.

"*There!*" Sister Clarice's voice thundered down on her like surf on a faraway beach, and her pointing finger hovered, blurred in Jilly's vision like a pink Zeppelin. "*There is the Penitential who dared to defy those the Lord set above her! Let her be made an example.*"

Rough hands hauled Jilly to her feet. "*Strip her!*" Sister Clarice's voice commanded. She had her riding crop clutched in one doughy hand.

Jilly came partway out of her daze when she felt hands start to tear at her clothes, writhing and kicking. But the male guards had her now, and the whites showed around their eyes.

"Help me!" she screamed to the watching slaves. "For the love of God, please help me! *It could be you next!*"

But they only looked away.

• • •

"There, there, poor dear," Brother Banner whispered throatily. He straightened and turned, fluttering his big soft hands at the other female slaves like white pigeons.

"Don't you girls have anything better to do than stand around and stare? If you aren't tired out yet, the Lord always needs strong legs to pedal for His glory."

The Penitentials shuffled back to their cots. Banner bent to smooth the cold wet towels Jilly held clamped between her welted inner thighs. She would not have pulled away even had she not been utterly drained, physically and spiritually. There was no more sexuality in Elder Brother Banner's touch than in a head nurse's.

"You poor child," he said. "They—no. I've gone far enough helping you like this, I can't set my judgment against the Lord's chosen Steward."

He leaned forward, kissed her chastely right beneath the ear, then bustled away to turn off the lights.

For what seemed hours she lay there tied into a fetal knot of misery, shivering. She heard the others stirring softly in their beds, heard a few cicada-buzzes of whispering that cut off sharply when Banner stuck his head back in to say, "Girls! If you have energy left to chat, you have energy to serve the Savior!"

In time she moved, very carefully; any slight friction set her buttocks and thighs afire again. She reached over the side of her cot. Her clothes had been dumped there in a heap. She rummaged in the pocket of the pants until she found the small packet she'd made of cloth torn from her shirt.

It was her hope chest, her compact with the future. Her commitment that someday she would be free, to return it for analysis to the Enclave labs.

It wasn't much. Only all she had. She pressed it to her cheek and finally slept.

"Well, Max," Jilly said, "don't think our time together hasn't been fun."

Two hours of working over the robot with Turtle Wax on the splintery pine floor had her knees in not much better shape than her rump. She didn't care. She had shined the strange dark alloy until she could see the distorted reflection of her face running like a squirrel over the vaulted archway of his

ribs. She had not done it for Coffin and the others, though
indeed to do less than a perfect job would be to invite another
whipping, or worse—the chosen of the Lord had an abrupt
way with repeat offenders. She had done it for herself—and
for Max.

Call it a labor of love.

She was clean, anyway, though laboring away in the morning
heat of the shed had made inroads into that. This morning she
had been permitted her first shower and shampoo since she was
taken prisoner. It would have been sheer ecstasy for her, even
though soapy water stung when it touched the welts Sister
Clarice's crop had left. But she had been haunted by an intuition
as to *why* she was being allowed to clean herself.

The intuition had crystallized into sick certainty when she
had finished toweling off in the shower block and unfolded the
clothes set out for her to wear: a red halter top and blue jeans
cut off so extremely that she felt convinced her currently puffy
buttcheeks must be on display like big wedges of Gorgonzola.

It made her sick to think about it. After going to such elab-
orate lengths to make sure she and the other female Penitentials
dressed as much like day laborers as possible, the Faithful
hadn't outfitted her like a Brood mama on spring break just
because they'd run out of decent clothes.

At least she'd been able to slip away from the shed once on
the pretext of needing some more scrubbing pads. Brother
Banner had let her paw through the used-clothing heap behind
the slave dorm until she found her old pants, had looked the
other way as she dug frantically in the pocket. She still had
her precious sample tucked away in a pocket of the skintight
cutoffs.

Quit fooling yourself, kid. She was never getting out of the
Fortress of Faith alive. She was going into the trailer to be the
Senior Steward's personal sex doll. When he was through he'd
probably pass her on to Buddy, all bloated and greasy, and
maybe when he'd had enough they'd let the defense forces
have a crack at her too. And one night when she couldn't take
it any longer she'd gnaw open the veins in her wrist.

She wouldn't be the first. The night-whisperers in the barracks made sure she knew that.

A tear fell on the gleaming skeletal stub of nose. She felt

the corresponding runlet of wetness along her own nose. She hadn't even known she was crying.

She leaned forward and gently kissed the cool slope of cheekbone, tasting her own salt on metal.

The eyes sunk deep in the alloy skull always reminded her of the ball-shape typing element of an ancient electric typewriter she'd seen at a technology exhibit in Los Alamos before the Valle Grande blew and turned what was left of the town into a castle surrounded by live-lava moats. Actually, they looked as she imagined a type-ball would look if you cut it in half and set one in each socket, cut side up.

Now she froze. She had the strangest sensation that those ruined eyes were *looking at her*.

"Max," she whispered, thinking, *so this is what it's like to completely and totally lose it*. "Max? Are you in there?"

"Say there, little darlin'," a voice said. "Hey there, hi there, ho there."

She squeaked, jumped and spun. "Prophet Buddy! You . . . you startled me. I didn't hear you coming."

Buddy beamed. He was dressed in his best: fresh laundered blue jeans, blue plaid work shirt, red and mustard Manzano High School Monarchs letter jacket. He took off his white straw cowboy hat with the fake peacock feather stuck in the band. Her nose twitched as a sudden astringent smell flooded the shed. It was just exactly like the disinfectant blocks they put in urinals in men's rooms—Jilly's most vivid memory of the one time she'd strayed into the wrong facility by accident, on a trip to see her horrible relatives in the hill country above Las Vegas, New Mexico. She guessed it emanated from the fistfuls of pomade he'd globbed on to slick back his blond hair.

"Just thought I'd stop on by and see how you were comin' with our metal friend there," Buddy said.

Yeah, sure, Jilly thought. She stood up warily. Reflexively she looked left and right of him, estimating her chances of darting past his bulk and out the door. But . . . to where? *No point in kidding yourself. There's no escape for you. Not ever*.

"You sure got a cute little butt!" he blurted. In two steps he was all over, arms crushing, hands groping, mouth working sloppily away at her neck and ear.

"Ooh, baby, c'mon," he gobbled, "you gonna purely *love* this."

The date-rape endearments were just too damn much. Jilly twisted her head and sank her teeth in his cheek like a ferret.

Buddy roared. His big hand smashed against the side of her head. It was like a bomb going off in her skull. She became aware of flying backward through the air in a vague sort of way, as if she were watching one of those special-effect films meant to make you think you were on a roller coaster or something. When her shoulders and the back of her head cracked into the wall of the shed it felt as if it was happening to someone else.

She slid in seeming slo-mo down the wall, tasting blood. Buddy loomed over her, and she saw a bloom of red on his cheek. That made her smile. Maybe it wasn't all *her* blood.

"You little cunt," Buddy slobbered, slurring his words in fury. He grabbed her by the front of the halter top and hauled her to her feet. She snapped back to herself and was afraid.

He saw the fear enter her. He smiled. "I'll teach you to mess with me, you Mexican whore. My whole body's a lethal weapon. I'm gonna beat the living shit out of you," he said, more steady now that his masculine confidence was bolstered by a shot of feminine fear. "Then I'm gonna fuck the shit out of you. Front, back, and sideways."

He cocked a meaty right fist, savoring her terror like wine. He'd never seen eyes that wide before. Except . . .

They seemed to be focused *beyond* him.

He wasn't about to fall for that one. Then he heard a rasp as of metal on wood. He glanced back, then he screamed.

Metal Max grabbed his right arm and tore it from the socket.

6

It is always night on the Pajarito Plateau.

A million years ago there was a giant mountain in the middle of what would one day be north central New Mexico. A million years ago, the top blew off. Falls of dust and ash from the explosion suffocated animals as far away as Nebraska.

What remained Spanish explorers named *el Valle Grande,* the Big Valley: a hole in the world, a gentle-sloped shallow bowl twelve miles by fifteen, furred with short, tough tan grass and dappled with drifting cloud shadows. Geologists called it the largest extinct volcano on earth.

Thirty months ago two gay priests from a monastery in nearby Jemez Springs were found parboiled in a hot spring not many miles west of the *caldera* or crater. The official explanation was that the two, whose blood showed alcohol content, had killed a bottle of wine, passed out, and stayed in the water too long.

Rumor said steam had vented into the spring from below, cooking both instantaneously.

Shortly thereafter travelers began to tell stories of strange

sounds and sights in the Jemez range around the perimeter of
the dead volcano, of weird rumblings, stirrings in the trees,
ghostly lights by night, sudden sulfurous stinks. Cowboys reported abrupt panic stampedes among the herds of cattle grazing
in the *Valle*.

The State Geologist's Office said it was all superstition and
rumor feeding on itself, like the cattle-mutilation crazes of the
late Twentieth Century.

*Pajarito means little bird. The little birds have returned. Life
has a way of doing that. Sometimes life pays the price: sometimes, along the slopes of the Plateau, you can find whole
flights of little birds all lying where a sudden venting of toxic
gas struck them dead.*

Twenty-five months ago all but three families of the Indians
who inhabited Jemez Pueblo packed up and moved to live with
their traditional allies, the Jicarilla Apache, on their reservation
near Dulce. They told reporters it was because the mountain
spirits were waking up again. A state welfare official who got
too zealous about insisting they return to their homes was
roughed up by men wearing kachina masks who bashed in the
windows of her station wagon with baseball bats.

Twenty-four months ago a team of geologists arrived from
the University of New Mexico in Albuquerque with a trailer
full of seismographic instruments. They claimed the old volcano was showing definite signs of life. The State Geologist's
Office accused them of publicity hunting.

Twenty-three months ago . . .

*Lava flows encircle the plateau. Most days they run at least
a trickle of live lava: the earth's life-blood, glowing red.*

Geologists had to admit to a slight miscalculation.

Valle Grande was the biggest *dormant* volcano on earth.

*The caldera is a gaping glowing wound. It shrouds the moun-
tains with a constant black curtain of ash and dense sulfur
stinking smoke. On a good day, the sun is visible as a wan
pink disk.*

Valle Grande announced its triumphant return engagement
with three thunderous cracks. The last was heard as far away
as Oregon. It was, in fact, the loudest sound anyone ever heard,
louder than Santorini or Rakatau, far louder than the biggest
thermonuclear firecracker humankind ever lit. Imagine gang-
firing the world's remaining stock of nukes.

All of them. At once. And double *that*.

The blasts simply wiped away the small town of Los Alamos, built on Pajarito Plateau east of the volcano. A glowing cloud, a hellstorm of poison gas and white-hot ash, swept down on Santa Fe like the scythe of the Angel of Death. Seventy miles down the Río Grande Valley the volcanoes west of Albuquerque reawakened in sympathetic eruptions, less spectacular but amply deadly.

The aboveground portions of the top-secret Los Alamos National Laboratory complex were destroyed by blast and pyroclastic flow. Much of the facility was subterranean, however, hardened to resist terrorist attack or thermonuclear near-misses. That hidden in the earth survived.

Like the birds, humans have returned to Pajarito Plateau. Indeed, they were never entirely dislodged.

Look close; there's one there now. . . .

She moved in a sinuous dance, her feet bare to the black pitted rock. The rock was a remnant of another spasm of tectonic temper, two thousand lifetimes ago by human standards, barely yesterday by the time span of the earth. The rock was warm beneath her callused soles, a warmth greater than the wan sun could account for—as if the long-dead lava remembered the wild violence of its birth and longed to flow free and hot and irresistible once more, like the molten rock that rumbled and seethed in glowing torrents around the base of the outcropping at the plateau's end.

She was naked. Her heavy brown hair was pulled back in a braid that slapped between the hard-muscled cheeks of her rump, sometimes in her *wushu* dance. Her skin was white, so pale it seemed to be daring the defeated sun to violate it. Freckles dusted her smoothly muscled shoulders and her nose, which was slightly snubbed. Her eyes at this moment were dark smoky blue with concentration.

Smoke tendrils slithered past her like climbing snakes. She ignored them. The flow of her movements changed, became less fluid and more forceful, as she commenced the stations of a North Chinese karate form. A watcher might have been startled by the strength the slim body displayed, spending blows on the air with speed and grace and precision. But there were no watchers.

She would have known.

No scars blemished the smooth perfect skin. There were no marks of any kind upon her. She was perfect.

A gold chain snugged around her waist, fine as a thought, was her only adornment, her only sign of compromise. She always wore the chain. It had been placed on her by the man who was more than her father, the man who tantalizingly refused to become her lover.

The man for whom she would kill anyone else on Earth.

She finished her kata. Facing outward across the river of dull gold fire she raised her arms from the sides, sweeping outward like the wings of a crane. Her pointed hands came together, rolled inward, drew into fists and pulled back down before her face and breasts to a hissing exhalation.

She brought her hands to her hips, then let her head fall forward, let the tension flow out of her.

For a moment she stood there, enjoying the sensuousness of the moment: her body abuzz with exercise, her mind concentrated yet relaxed, the soft pressure of sun on freckled shoulders and the braid down her back and the bite of sulfur smoke, the black frozen sponge underfoot, the heat and light and angry ceaseless mutter of the molten rockstream.

She raised her face slowly, brushed back a few vagrant strands of hair with both hands. She shuddered then, and turned to go.

Below her a gas bubble broke the surface, burst. Glowing gobbets of rocks splashed upward like the earth's hot jism.

One struck her small right breast, a fingerbreadth below the brown aureole. She gasped, and her lips skinned back from her teeth. She stood a moment, legs slightly apart, head back, fists knotted.

The lava gurgled. Slowly her features ran the spectrum from pain to pleasure.

She smiled. She tweaked the nipple of the injured breast lightly with her fingers and laughed aloud. She stroked her fingertips down the breast's underside.

As she started the treacherous climb to the plateau's top the red mark the lava spatter had left was fading.

7

Forever after Jilly would remain convinced that between the instant Buddy Coffin's arm, still in its letter jacket sleeve with the football patches on it, tore away with an indescribable sound and the first geyser of blood, there was an endless awful moment in which *nothing happened*.

She would never know whether it was the diastole pause before systole's spasmic pulse or just the circuit breakers tripping behind her frightened eyes. But for a pocket eternity they held that tableau, Jilly pinned against the shed wall by terror and disbelief like a dead thing for drying, Buddy staring at the place he inexplicably came to an end, Metal Max looming behind him with a skull's bland grin, dangling Buddy's arm casually from one metallic hand.

Buddy's blood hit the shed's far wall at the same instant his scream hit Jilly's eardrums. Time started again.

Buddy collapsed thrashing and wailing, his blood rushing out of him like crowds from a burning theater. The right side of the metal skeleton she had polished with such care was speckled with fine blood dots, rich dark purple-red in the shed light. As she watched they began to run into a network of fine lines.

Max stretched out his free hand to her.

She cringed away. *Monster!* She feared him more than she had ever feared Buddy. More than she could ever fear Buddy.

Voices rose outside. They had the tone of people asking questions they already knew they did not want answered. Buddy's first shriek of pain had been startlingly shrill, but there was no way such a sound could have issued from Jillian Romero's slim body. It was like the bellow of a bullcalf when he feels the castrator's knife on the base of his scrotum.

The ruined type ball eyes flickered toward the open shed door, back to her. The lower jaw moved up and down in a macabre parody of speech. No sound came. The monster froze, cocked its head in a pantomime of surprise.

A hysterical laugh clawed for Jilly's throat. She fought it off. But at that almost-comical gesture something changed in her as to the closing of a switch.

She had thought she was in the presence of a monster from a B-movie or a science fiction novel: a berserker, a Terminator, a soulless machine created for one purpose alone—killing humans. But somehow she understood that whatever the being she thought of as Max was, he was not a machine.

Or not *just* a machine.

Buddy was subsiding to a gasping sobbing moan. Again Max gestured with his hand, urgently now. She pushed off from the wall, moving toward the door, keeping as far from him as she could. She could not bring herself to come within touching range if she could help it.

A skinny balding Brother in sky-blue coveralls appeared in the doorway. He looked right past Max at the blood-drenched form rolling on the floor.

"Omigod," he gasped. "*Prophet Buddy!*"

Then his brain finally finished processing the data his eyes were sending it, and he stared Max full in his metal face and shrieked.

Max put his palm in the middle of the sunken chest and pushed. The Brother took off as if he were strapped to a rocket pack, landing on his butt in a whirlwind of dust.

Max stepped into the late-morning sunlight. Cautiously Jilly followed.

The compound was full of people going about the Lord's business, voluntarily or otherwise. At the sight of Metal Max they stopped in midstride as if turned to stone.

"It's the Devil!" a chicken-necked Sister shrilled. *"It's the Devil made all shiny metal!"* A forager dropped his rifle and fell to his knees to weep for the Lord to help him, sour terrified vomit slopping over his thin lips to improve the camouflage pattern of his K-mart-surplus shirt.

Metal Max turned his head left and right, surveying the hilltop planed by bulldozers and constant wind, the prefab barracks and trailers, the road unrolling down the slope to the right, the wire mesh fence conveniently near, just ahead.

The alloy skull tracked farther left, and back, and back. The robot—or whatever he was—stared up for a long moment at Christ made manifest in shatter-resistant plastic, a hundred twenty-five feet tall, arms spread in benediction, standing before rank upon unoccupied rank of exercise bikes wired up to serve as manpowered generators and fixed to badly poured cement slabs.

"What in God's name is going on here?" a voice demanded from upslope. The lordly bulk of the Supreme Steward himself had appeared at the corner of the refectory and chapel.

The Brother Max had sent flying had finally managed to fit some air back in his chest. "It's Satan his own self!" he slobbered, flinging a scarecrow arm to point at Max. "He kilt Prophet Buddy!"

"Romero! You greasy little bitch, you brought this down upon us!" Jilly turned to see Sister Clarice bearing down on her like a soft iceberg in a salmon dress with sweatstains under the arms. "This is all your doing! I'll see you sizzle in hell!"

She whipped up a hand. Jilly flinched, remembering the surprising speed and strength of Clarice's huge doughy arms and the bite of her riding crop. But the woman was out of reach, still a good fifteen feet away.

Sunlight glinted on bright nickel finish. You could never tell what a woman like Sister Clarice might be hiding beneath her voluminous skirts. She had a stubby little semiauto pistol in her hand. Pointed right at Jilly.

The pistol's black eye flashed yellow. Max's left hand darted out, interposing. Jilly saw it jerk as the bullet struck it and was deflected, singing as it tumbled away across the wind.

Belying her bulk Clarice danced to the side, craning the gun, trying to get a shot past the robot into Jilly's smooth brown skin. Max shifted smoothly as a ballet dancer, trying to keep himself between the Sister and the girl.

Clarice skinned purple lips back from her teeth and fired again. Jilly squealed and ducked as a hot breath brushed her cheek.

Max hit Sister Clarice with the bloody end of Buddy Coffin's arm. Right between the eyes. It made a sound like a jack-o'-lantern knocked off a counter onto the kitchen floor.

Max drew the arm back like a club, ready for a follow-up blow. Sister Clarice had a self-absorbed look to her. At least her eyes were rolled up and kind of together, as if she were trying to stare at the bloody dent in her forehead. She dropped stiffly to her knees, then went over in the dust like a tranquilized elephant.

Max jerked his head for Jilly to precede him. Downhill to the wire. She sidled past, still reluctant to put herself where he could actually touch her.

Zephaniah Coffin, Minister Plenipotentiary for the Kingdom of Heaven and All Like That, raised his eyes to the sky and tore his reddish-black beard.

"In the name of Christ who watches all and weeps," he wailed in his airhorn voice, "will no one step forth to avenge my sister's poor son and our brave Sister Clarice?"

The ground burned Jilly's feet through the tire rubber soles of her sandals, and hot khaki dust washed between the sandals and her feet. Max's footsteps crunched behind her, methodic and unhurried. She was starting to feel numb again when somebody danced by to square off between her and the perimeter wire.

"Stop right there, Penitential Sister Romero," Skip Coffin stammered over the black barrel of a port-arms M-16. "Don't go no—any further."

"Skip," she said. It felt as if her mouth had been packed with sawdust, as if she had to push each word on its way with her tongue. "Hunk. Get out of the way. *Please*. You don't know what you're doing."

He went another shade paler and blinked at the hair trailing sweat-wet ends in his eyes. "I do know, right enough. I'm doing what's right. For Amos and the Lord."

She heard the squeal of pebbles crushed by a metal foot. Max swept past her like a gust of wind off the desert.

Hosea Coffin, the boy who would be Hunk, was scared and green and kind of a nerd, but he was quick enough. He got the assault rifle down and squeezed a burst right into the middle of the gleaming metal ribcage as the robot charged.

There was a world of difference between *quick enough* and *good enough*. Jilly screamed and covered her ears as noise and ricocheting bullets splashed past her. Then Max had grabbed the rifle by its flash suppressor and plucked it right out of the boy's hands.

He raised it, preparing to drive the butt and most of Skip's teeth right out the back of the young man's head. Without thinking Jilly threw herself at him, grabbed him by the arm. His metal skeleton was unyielding. Despite the dazzling sunlight it felt cold. Colder than the grave.

"*No!*" she screamed. "Don't hurt him! He doesn't know any better!"

Skip was wringing his right hand with his left. Trigger or guard must have busted his forefinger when the rifle was torn away. Despite the pain and sheer panic twisting his young face, he held his ground.

Max handed him his brother's arm.

By reflex Skip clutched it to his chest. Then he stared at it as if he'd never seen it before. He screamed, threw the arm spastically away, and hit the hardpan in a fetal curl.

A gunshot cracked. Jilly heard the answering crack of the bullet passing by. She flinched, ducked almost to one knee.

The smoke and unburned propellant of Skip's short burst had stained the front of Max's metal chest, and thereby done a lot more damage than the jacketed bullets had. Unless the Fortress Faithful had antitank rockets, they weren't going to be able to make much of an impression on the robot, by the looks of things. Absolved of worrying for the safety of her terrifying benefactor, Jilly was free to concentrate on the fact that even Max's inhuman speed and agility could never prevent the crazies from shooting her to pieces. There were just too many of them, too spread out—and she had presence of mind to marvel at how tactically the last two years had taught her to think, and how appalled her poor parents would be.

The sentry by the gate fired again. He was either slow on

the uptake or none too accurate; his round crashed off Max's right shoulder, rocking the robot slightly.

Max took hold of the pistol grip of Skip's M-16 and brought the rifle around one-handed, like an outsized pistol. *Jeez Louise,* Jilly thought, *maybe he's not programmed how to shoot.*

"His eyes!" a Sister wailed. "Lord Gawd, his eyes is a glowin' red! Godamercy on us all!"

Max fired a single shot. Dust puffed from the sentry's shirt-front. He dropped his rifle, stepped back and toppled into the razor-wire loop drawn across the road.

The gunshot echoed up the canyon and for a moment there was only the wind and the pressure of dozens of frightened eyes.

Max tracked his weapon back up the hill to where Coffin had been standing a heartbeat before. The Senior Prophet's bulk had vanished without trace. Zephaniah Coffin was clearly a man who believed the Lord looked out for those who looked out for themselves.

Movement plucked at the periphery of Jilly's vision. "Look out!" she screamed. "The statue—"

Metal Max had already started his motion, swinging the rifle right while shifting to interpose himself between Jilly and the two Faithful who had popped into view around the far corner of the Christ of the Sandias' podium. One levered shots from a Winchester while the other hosed bullets from waist level from some kind of stubby machine pistol. Jilly heard the rounds pass overhead with a sound like sheets tearing.

For a millisecond Jilly thought she could see red dots on the bib-overall chest of the man with the machine pistol. Max fired twice, *pow-pow,* as fast as the 16 would cycle. He switched the barrel farther upslope with micrometric precision, fired once at the Winchester boy, who had stopped and was standing spread-legged and red-faced screaming as he emptied his own tubular magazine.

He was falling before his buddy's body hit dirt.

Max turned to the wire. He raised his left arm.

Nothing happened.

He rotated his left arm to look at the forearm's inside. The way he pulled his head back when he saw the empty housing turned Jilly's flesh to ice inside her sunwarmed skin all over again.

Bullets kicked up a flurry of dust around Jilly's feet and rang off Max's alloy bones like windchimes on crack. Max went to one knee with the impacts. Jilly screamed.

The robot pointed downslope with his free hand, made shooing gestures at Jilly when she didn't take right off. She got it then, raced down to just inside the wire and went belly-down in the hot hard dirt as another burst raked the earth where she'd been standing.

"Fire Base Charlie, this is OP Medfly, over."

"Go ahead, Medfly, over."

"Fire Base Charlie, we are reporting activity in Fort Jesus, over."

"What kind of activity, Medfly, over?"

"We have shots fired, and some kind of pretty vigorous activity. We can't see exactly what's going on, but them Fortress Fatheads're carrying on like old J.C.'s trying to uproot his feet so's he can hike on down to the Lota Burger. Over."

"Say again, Medfly, over."

"I say there's something happening up inside the wire. Shooting and some kind of rumble. Hold on—what the fuck? Yeah, Lucian says maybe it's a breakout."

"Medfly, can you confirm breakout? How many are involved, over?"

"Negative, Charlie, it's unclear what the heck is going on. Don't look like a big rush for the exits or nothing. Wait—more shots, we have semi- and full-auto fire coming from inside the wire again."

"Medfly, are you receiving fire, over?"

"Negative on the incoming, Charlie. They're keeping it in the wire. But whatever it is, it sure sounds serious. Uh, Charlie, if it is a breakout, do we assist the escapees, over?"

"Negative on that, Medfly. I say again, negative on assistance. If you can confirm breakout, call in and await orders, but under no circumstances take action to aid or hinder an escape attempt without specific instructions. Do you copy, Medfly, over?"

"Blowjob."

"Say again, Medfly, over?"

"Just clearing my throat. Uh, roger, Charlie, we copy. No move without further—hold on, hold on now. Something—somebody running right at the wire, right in our direction—hoo doggie, looks like a girl. What, she thinks she's gonna just climb out? Cut herself to ribbons on the razor tape up top. More shots—here, somebody else running this way, into the wire. What, does he have armor? He looks—

"Great Christ Almighty on a skateboard, will you take a look at that?"

With the same machine-tool precision—not seeming to hurry, yet eye-blurring fast—as every other move he had made, Max straightened and turned back to face uphill. A soldier of the Lord was standing up on the flat roof of the chapel/refectory, firing an ancient H&K 91 from the shoulder. The 91 fired full-sized 7.62 millimeter ammunition, too big for full-auto fire to be any kind of accurate, which was why Jilly Romero wasn't kicking and spurting the last of her life into the thirsty gray dust.

The second burst cracked past Max. He thumbed the selector to full auto as he swung the M-16 up. For some reason nobody had ever disabled the three-round burst regulator. Even hurrying the shot he didn't need more.

He was sprinting the rest of the distance to the wire as the H&K man spun, fell heavily to hit the parapet with his hip, and dropped with a crunch to the ground. Max passed Jilly, went to one knee hard inside the fence and gestured urgently at her.

Looking back at him over her shoulder, Jilly's first thought was, *you've* got *to be kidding!* Another bullet from somewhere kicked dust stingingly into one cheek. She jumped up and ran right at the robot.

He set down the rifle to make a stirrup of his hands. *This is really crazy,* she thought. She socketed her foot into the alloy hands without breaking stride.

She pushed off with all her strength as he straightened. It wasn't necessary; she knew at once he could have bodily tossed her over the three-meter fence unassisted if he had to. A razor-wire loop caressed her right calf, laying a needle-line of red across the smooth brown skin. A moment of free fall, heart in her throat, and she was dropping toward the ground at a really alarming rate.

She'd had some gymnastics as a little girl, continuing until she dislocated a hip doing splits in eighth grade. They didn't really help. She did have the presence of mind to curl herself into a ball and tuck her head, which meant she didn't break anything when the planet hit her. It did knock all the air out of her, and she went rolling down the slope, unraveling from her ball, arms and legs everywhere, bouncing off rocks and the mounds dirt made where it drifted at the base of the bunch-grass and raising a big bow-wave of dust.

Behind her Metal Max put both his hands in the stout wire mesh and pulled. It parted like cheesecloth. He stooped to snag the black rifle by its sling, and ran down after the tumbling girl.

8

Jilly collapsed on the gray-weathered splintery wood. "I can't go another step," she panted, hanging her head between bare scuffed knees. "It feels as if I'm breathing acid. I don't care if they catch us." Even as she spoke she knew that wasn't true. But the strength had been wrung out of her.

It had been a tract home, recycled fiberboard and plastic glass, with plastic novelty statuary on pressboard shelves above the formica bar and Jesus and Elvis side by side on the wall, made manifest in black velvet. If the natural cycle of things held true, it would be again. For generations they had been building them here, the throwaway homes, replacing them like pairs of old socks when the patches wouldn't hold together any more. Boxes to keep the permanent floating underclass in. The paid minstrels of the American élite, who lived by passing tax money squeezed out of the proletariat to one another, sang disparagingly about *ticky-tacky*, but their patrons kept writing zoning and rent-control laws to keep the dirty-neck masses from moving in next to *them*.

The houses down the hill from the Fortress of Faith had been of a much better class, at least up to a couple of years ago. Foothills property had been at a premium, and the expensive split-level homes with their clerestory windows and solar-powered hot tubs had marched up into the Sandias until they collided with the boundary of Cibola National Forest. They had been premium targets for looters, too, after Eruption made a final mockery of already-failing attempts to preserve social order.

Now there was a buffer zone of derelict houses around the Fortress of Faith, like the hulks of yachts beached and decaying on the wet-sand margin between land and sea. Beyond that lay the domain of Councilman DiStefano, well-armed and well-guarded.

Jilly had wanted *out of there* at all costs. There had been no visible sign of pursuit from the hilltop as Max hauled her to her feet and into the dead zone of abandoned houses, but there would be as soon as Reverend Coffin levered his gross bulk out of whatever hole he'd stuffed it down and began to harangue some backbone back into the Faithful. *Especially* when he saw what the robot had left of Prophet Buddy.

She had led Metal Max south and west in wordless but controlled panic. Now frenzied exertion and the now-midday sun that had been slamming her on the head and shoulders like a lead pipe whenever they strayed out of the all-too-infrequent shade were exacting their toll.

She began to be aware of the abrasions and tiny cuts, not to mention tumbleweed bristles and goathead thorns, she had picked up on her roll down Mt. Zion. She sighed and began to pick various spines out of her long legs.

A sound of metal on dry earth and dead grass. She came into a crouch, ready to dart away. Max came into the back yard with Skip's M-16 held casually across his hips in what Jilly had come to recognize these past two years as patrol position.

For a moment she poised, suspended between her fear of the robot and her fear of where she'd be without him. After a few heartbeats she settled back with a sigh. Whatever he was, she owed her life to him.

He looked at her with those type-ball eyes. She tried not to shiver.

"I wish I could talk to you," she said. She was beginning

to reel in her breath, though now her throat was crackling-dry for lack of water. "No, I guess I can *talk* to you all I want. But you can't talk to me, and I can't even tell if you know what I'm saying."

He pointed past her. She jumped and spun, afraid she'd see a rattler curled on the deck behind her or a scorpion sneaking up on her bare flank.

It took a moment to see and accept what was there: "HELLO," in pale red that quivered slightly on the sand-colored stucco wall.

She looked from the word to Max. Red gleams shone from the depths of his eyes. A few vagrant dust motes flashed red in a line between eyes and word.

"Wow! You're doing that with a laser of some kind, aren't you? Like a laser light show?"

Max nodded.

"I didn't know you could do that."

The alloy jaw moved up and down. "NEITHER DID I," the light wrote.

She found herself edging away from him. *Watch yourself, girl*. Breaking the bubble of communication had upset her equilibrium. She was veering dizzily between giddy trust and mind-breaking terror of the metal man.

"Who are you?" she asked, eyes flicking rapidly back and forth between him and the wall.

"MY NAME IS . . ."

The glowing words vanished. She waited. Several seconds passed, then: "DONOVAN STEELE."

Jilly frowned at him. "Why the hesitation? Glitch in your programming?"

"IN A MANNER OF SPEAKING."

"But Steele's really your name?"

"YES. WHAT'S YOURS?"

"Sorry. I think some of my manners got left behind when the crazies snatched me." She brushed a strand of black hair back from her face. "My name is Jillian Romero, Mr. Steele. I'm very pleased to meet you. Thanks for rescuing me."

"MY PLEASURE, MS. ROMERO."

She laughed at the incongruity of it, then cut the laugh off flat before it got out of hand. Her mood was very fragile, and this was not the time to start coming apart. "Jilly. Call me Jilly."

"JILLY, WE SHOULD BE MOVING SOON. HAVE YOU CAUGHT YOUR BREATH?"

She nodded, stood. He turned to lead the way.

"Just a minute," she said, hanging back. "There's something I have to know. I can't think of any real graceful way to put it, so I'll just blurt it out: Are you a man or a machine?"

He stood looking at her for a long moment. Something in his posture struck her as immeasurably sad. Pinpoints of red appeared in his eyes.

"I'M A MAN." The words danced on the wall.

"I THINK."

"This is kind of no-man's-land," she explained, crouching in the angle between a gutted Circle K convenience store and a bullet-riddled dumpster waiting to see what was making the motor sounds coming north on Juan Tabo, which she pronounced "Wan Tuh-*bow*." "North of us is Dino DiStefano's territory, south of the freeway belongs to Barbara Brand."

The freeway in question was Interstate 40, which cut northwest across town from the mouth of Tijeras Canyon. It ran about half a kilometer south of them. She had been leading Max—no, Steele—parallel to it since their backyard rest break.

"WHO ARE DiSTEFANO AND BRAND? GANG LEADERS?"

She laughed. "Sort of. They belong to the City Council. They say they run the city. Actually, each of 'em runs a piece of it, and spends most of his or her time trying to figure out how to screw the others.

"This particular stretch belongs to nobody—or maybe everybody. Gangs—real gangs—and transients, mostly. A little farther on and we'll have to skirt the outpost the people from Kirtland keep in the old Reserve Center on Wyoming."

"KIRTLAND?" glowed on the cinder block wall.

"Military base south of town." She darted a quick look through the space between the dumpster and the building, which was set at a forty-five degree angle to the street, south along Juan Tabo.

"Speaking of the dreaded Blue Berets," she said, pulling back in a hurry, "here they come now."

An armored car was rolling north on big cleated tires made of honeycomb plastic that never went flat and supposedly wouldn't burn. The helmeted head of the driver stuck out the top of the one-man turret. The stub barrel of an automatic grenade launcher and the longer, slimmer proboscis of a coaxial machinegun jutted from the turret's front. On the side of the sharp-angled bow was lettered HELL ON FOUR WHEELS.

"MILITARY?" the glowing temporary graffiti asked. "AMERICAN MILITARY?"

Jilly nodded. "We've been part of the Union for a couple centuries now, though Mexico makes noises about taking us back every once in a while. I think we'd have to ask *real* nice, the way things are now."

"SHOULD I FLAG THEM DOWN? THEY COULD PROBABLY DO A BETTER JOB OF KEEPING YOU SAFE THAN I CAN."

She laughed bitterly. "Maybe you should just take me back to Mt. Zion now. If I pretended I was real enthusiastic I might be able to make the Senior Prophet forget how you pulled the arm off his favorite nephew. Or maybe I can convince him you abducted me against my will."

Steele looked at her. "YOU'RE AFRAID OF THE MILITARY?"

"I'll put it this way: I won't have to spread myself quite so *thin* back up with the Bikers for Jesus. The Rev would keep me to himself until he got tired of me, and then probably pass me on to Skip. And what the heck? I mean, Skip's almost cute, and I could probably get used to calling him Hunk a lot sooner than I could learn to really *relax* with a couple of hundred of our boys in uniform I haven't been properly introduced to."

She pressed her back flat against the wall of the convenience store, trying to make herself one with the shadows that were beginning to grow as the sun started down the sky. The next lot was a half-meter higher than the Circle K, with a cinderblock retaining wall to make up the difference, and between that and the tumbleweeds and trash that had drifted against the back of the building she guessed they were safe from observation. The car cruised north, apparently oblivious.

"Not much of anybody cares for the Enclave, Mr. Steele. Not the City Council, not the flyboys at the base. We refuse to play their power games, and so far we've been too mean for anybody to crush us. So they take it out on us any way they can.''

There were few signs of habitation along the route she led him. The Enclave lay about two-thirds of the distance from foothills to river. She explained that she was keeping them near the boundary of Councilwoman Brand's territory, which was the loosest-held of any of the areas claimed by city councilors, except for her stronghold in Four Hills, well away from their line of march. Occasionally they saw signs of normal civilian traffic north of them. It had a rapid, furtive nature, like the inhabitants of a prairie dog village, ready to bolt for their holes at the warning bark of a sentry or the telltale flashing passage of the shadow of hawk's wings.

Most of the homes showed little damage beyond what the elements—mostly sun and wind—had done in two years of neglect. There were frequent signs of vandalism and minor looting—windows broken, doors forced by foragers or transients looking for a place to stay. What few vehicles remained had been thoroughly stripped.

Every now and then they would encounter the burnt-out shell of a house, and once they took refuge from a sudden muffled stutter of gunfire to the south in the backyard of a home whose garage-become-den was just plain flattened as if Godzilla had stepped on it.

"Volcanic bomb," Jilly explained. "Once in a while a live crater spits out a big glob of molten rock. Sometimes it's a bubble of poison gas, sometimes it's pretty solid. This was probably a gas bomb. They cool in flight. Solids hold enough heat to torch the place, probably take down half the block."

Twice Steele tensed and pulled Jilly into cover, and twice little knots of ragged, skinny foragers came into view immediately after. The first—two men and a woman, Jilly thought, though it was hard to tell with a rifle and a bullpup shotgun in view—cruised right down the block within twenty meters of their lie-up behind the blowing wind-shredded curtains of what had been a sliding glass door. The second group was four strong, with only a single long arm showing; they crossed the far end of the block and disappeared, and Jilly had the distinct impression that they had caught sight of her and her companion.

It made sense that the dirtballs would want to avoid any

interaction that might turn loud and protracted. Jilly and Steele weren't all that far from the boundary between DiStefano's turf and Maynet's, and if you threw in the base and Brand—each constantly picking at the others for signs of weakness, and jealously guarding against his neighbors' probes—no party was going to want for crashers very long. Smash-and-grab and, where possible, the odd quiet throat-slitting was the style in this part of town.

Half a klick from the house trashed by the volcanic bomb, their path crossed a broad east-west artery called Lomas. As they raced across engines snarled to the west. They ran flat out—at least Jilly did; she had the impression Steele held up so as not to leave her behind—and went to ground in a former dart-supply store as ten or a dozen motorcycles swept past. Big chopped Harleys, riders rangy and well-armed.

Steele looked at Jilly. She had told him they were swinging well north to avoid the Kirtland outpost in the Reserve Center. The gang had clearly ridden within half a long block of the military post.

She shrugged. "Road Weasels," she said. "*Nobody* screws with them."

To save distance Jilly wanted them to cross I-40 where it cut Wyoming on a transverse slash; you didn't want to try running across the freeway proper. It was too wide and open, and the power players—the five councilors and the base— respected a semi-truce with each other there. Everybody else was fair game. In the last six months work gangs from the various factions had been permitted by mutual if unspoken consent to clear the scrubby desert vegetation from the right-of-way margins, to keep the dirtballs from ambushing patrols and trade convoys.

It was a risky place to cross. Only the embankment for the overpass where Wyoming crossed 40 hid them from direct view of the Reserve Center, several hundred meters south past the four former car dealerships that sprawled around the intersection of Wyoming and Lomas like the lost graveyard of a race of giant metal beetles. But fatigue and stress and lack of water in this merciless sun were beginning to get to Jilly. Her feet dragged when she moved, and her tongue dragged when she spoke.

Before they got to the overpass they heard the popcorn-

popping sound of a firefight breaking out some distance north.
They dodged into an abandoned animal hospital where windows
like inconveniently high firing slits bled afternoon light into a
side corridor that still smelled faintly of disinfectant and sick
animals.

A siren had begun to keen at the Reserve Center. By standing
on tiptoe Jilly found she could peer out one of the window
slits. The glass block, pitted by dust storms and the occasional
fall of abrasive volcanic ash, blurred her vision, but she could
still see well enough to recognize the vehicles screaming north:
a pair of Hummers, another armored car, a canvasback truck
painted in splotches of tan and brown and buff, crammed with
troopies in coalscuttle plastic helmets clutching plastic rifles.

She glanced nervously at Steele. "Should we be hanging
out here? What if a foot patrol comes by?"

"IT WON'T. FIGHTING'S TOO FAR NORTH. THESE
PEOPLE STRIKE ME AS THE KIND NEVER TO WALK
WHEN THEY CAN RIDE."

She pushed a laugh through her nose. "You got that right."

She turned and slid down with her back to the wall. It felt
as if her body belonged to someone else.

She was asleep before her rump touched ancient linoleum.

_9_

The man looked up from the end of a runway of linen so white it practically reflected his pale ascetic features. ''You're late.''

There was only one other chair in the dining hall, at the far end of the long table from the man, who wore a summerweight suit scarcely less blindingly white than the tablecloth. The young woman snagged the chair casually in passing, dragged it to the far end of the table, sat in it with slim powerful legs crossed and one sandaled foot brushing the man's shin, as if by accident.

The man took no notice. It was just one of the little games they played.

He continued to eat vegetable broth. His spoon never kissed the bone-white porcelain of the bowl. He was a small man, precisely controlled his movements and appearance, who gave the impression of sparing sounds as grudgingly as he would emotions.

He did not repeat the charge, nor did he look at her. She liked to play dress-up; now she was wearing what she thought of as her gypsy outfit: flaring colorful skirt, simple lightweight white blouse, strands of beads at necklace and wrists that made jittery jangles as she moved. Her long dark hair was held back by a garish bandanna tied around her head.

She leaned far forward, far enough that even a casual glance would have shown the man a small cone-shaped breast peeking out of the blouse, which was quite diaphanous to begin with. The man didn't spare a glance. The young woman shifted in her seat. The slit skirt fell open as if by accident, baring a dart of crossed leg clear to the hip. The man's eyes never left his soup.

The room was paneled in dark wood and echoingly dark. What light there was seemed mostly provided by the three candles placed in cut-glass holders at intervals on the long table. The small flame-shaped bulbs in their wrought-iron sconces spaced along the walls barely cast a glow as far as the paneling behind them.

Except for the blackness that seemed to press in like physical weights on the tiny domes of candlelight, there was nothing to. indicate the dining chamber lay a hundred meters beneath the tormented surface of the planet.

The woman shifted in her chair again. She wrinkled her nose petulantly. The air conditioning worked with an incessant white-noise hum that most people tuned out instantly. She was aware of it, as she was aware of the smell of disinfectant from the internal air-system filters, and of the mildew that formed on them in spite of chemical treatment and constant replacement. She was even aware of a mephitic tint that the hydrostatic precipitators couldn't scrub from the air brought in from outside. She was aware of all her surroundings, vividly and immediately.

She could smell herself as well. That irritated her; she'd just gotten out of the shower. Her desire for this man who would barely look at her was making itself known. She shifted back away from him. He had nostrils almost as acute as hers and disapproved strongly of bodily smell of any kind. The way she smelled was one of the few things she was self conscious about.

"I had to shower," she said. Her voice was contralto, a bit husky from breathing volcanic smoke.

"You could barely tell," the man said. "You smell like a polecat."

She flushed. "I was doing my forms. Out at the end of the plateau, above the lava flows."

That got his attention. His ice-pale eyes snapped up to hers. She smirked. She had a smile of incredible sweetness, a smile da Vinci would have booted the moon-faced wife of his *pro tem* patron downstairs to capture in oils.

"It's dangerous," he said.

"I was made to live dangerously," she purred, clasping her hands coyly around her knee.

"You weren't made to waste a decade's effort on an accidental fall into molten lava." His words rapped like knuckles on the tabletop. "I have forbidden it."

"You never let me do what I want," she said, undergoing a phase shift from kittenish to sulky in the time it took an atom to decay.

"What you want doesn't enter into it." He wiped his mouth with his napkin.

"Very well," he said, sitting up straight in his chair. "I have resisted this conclusion as long as possible. You've grown impossible to control. I regret what I must do, but I feel it's better to start over from scratch rather than risk the entire operation. I learned the lessons my rivals at Project Steele seemed so unable to absorb."

The door at the chamber's far end slid open. Four men stepped in. They wore camouflage smocks with sidearms belted over them and red berets bearing the emblem of the Los Alamos National Laboratories.

The compact man in white looked up at them, nodded. "Gentlemen."

He looked to the woman, who was lounging in the chair with one arm cocked over the back of it, the personification of *casual*.

"Attend me carefully, Misericordia, dear," he said. She tipped her head to look at him. "They are the handpicked élite of our fine LANL security detachment. They are more than that. Each of them has received a download of the combat skills that once belonged to Lt. Donovan Steele of the NYPD Strike Force."

"The crazy cyborg." She plucked the single white rose from its bud vase in front of the man and began to twirl its head beneath her nose.

"The pride of our rivals. The ultimate melding of machine and man."

She laughed.

The four men had moved forward and arranged themselves in a semicircle around the young woman. The one with a sergeant's black chevrons on the shoulder of his cammie smock placed himself between her and the man in white.

"We're at your disposal, Dr. James," he said.

"I've been through those downloads too," she said, sounding bored. "That's all a crock anyway, you know. No download can give you the muscle memory you need to improve physical performance in any big way. Besides, you'd have to be exactly Steele's body type to integrate it. Otherwise it's like using Porsche 9-Mega reflexes to drive a semi."

"We do pretty well for ourselves, Ms. Misericordia," said the black one, who stood to her right.

She smiled at him. "It's just 'Misericordia.'"

Dr. James dabbed his mouth with his napkin and folded it and his hands in his lap. "Sgt. Belasco," he said, "arrest Misericordia, take her out the South Portal, and shoot her. I cannot deal with her any longer."

Belasco stiffened, moistened his lips. "I'm sorry, uh, Misericordia. Dr. James is in charge, and in the current state of emergency that gives him what we call, uh, plenary police powers. We're going to have to do what he says."

She tipped her head back and showed him her most beautiful smile. "It doesn't mean we can't be friends."

She rolled her hips counterclockwise in the chair. The skirt, which was slit to the waist, fell open. A wedge of dark pubic hair showed between the slim pale thighs.

These men were good. They were very good. But they were healthy aggressive males, and the Steele download only augmented that.

It was the one on the black security man's left, just behind her right shoulder, who responded most. She smelled it in his sweat, heard it in the catch in his breathing. She traversed her smile to bear on him and fired her chair backward with a savage thrust of her legs. Its back hit him in the front of his left thigh as her elbow slammed into his balls. He doubled across her with a squealing gasp.

Her left hand shot up, and she felt a surge of ecstasy as the stiffened fingers penetrated the skin stretched over the vee of his jaw's underside. She cranked her hips, using her hold on his jaw and a fistful of fly to add to his forward motion and threw him across her, pinwheeling into Belasco and taking him down in a tangle of arms and legs.

The two still on their feet grabbed for their sidearms with Download enhanced reflexes. Misericordia slid down to the polished hardwood floor. She scythed her legs, cutting the black security man's legs out from under him as his handgun cleared the holster.

She doubled like an eel, grabbing his gun arm by the forearm as he fell, controlling it so his elbow cracked hard on the floor. His fingers, momentarily numbed, relaxed. She threw herself across him, whipping the pistol from his grasp.

In less than a heartbeat he was on top of her, cursing as he grabbed for the gun. She reversed it, thrust it into his solar plexus, and pulled the trigger.

He bellowed. She tangled fingers in the front of his camouflage smock and rolled onto her back, drawing his greater bulk over on top of her. The fourth security man had his weapon out now, leveled into a Weaver combat stance, hoping to get a clear shot at her.

Blood was erupting out of the man she'd gutshot, soaking her blouse, making her knuckles and the weapon slippery. She twisted the pistol to bear on the man trying to draw a bead on her, fired through the squirming body of his comrade.

The issue sidearm was a heavy semiauto Smith & Wesson 10mm piece. Combat firearms are called on to do two things: defeat body armor, and transmit enough of a shock to make the target lose interest in further annoying the shooter. Because no handgun produces all that much energy compared to a rifle or a shotgun, this tends to be an either/or proposition. More velocity to increase penetration means a smaller round and less of what is mistakenly called "knockdown power"; increased shock means a larger, and thus slower, slug. The powerful 10mm and sister .40 caliber rounds won rapid and near-universal acceptance at the tail end of the Twentieth Century because they offered near-optimal compromise between the 9mm's penetration and the one-shot-stop potential of a .45 ACP.

Science had marched right along since then, as usual.

The round Misericordia blasted through the security man was soft lead contained in a paper-thin polyceram jacket, with a concave tip for easy expansion. Like any hollowpoint it would expand uselessly on body armor—which was what the Teflon-coated tool-steel penetrator, four millimeters in diameter and sharp as a needle, *inside* the softer slug was for. The round expanded as advertised, failing to exit his body and making a hell of a mess in there.

The penetrator punched out his back, still moving at a pretty good clip, and hit the man with the pistol about two inches above the clasp of his web belt. It sprayed the whole front of him with a mist of tiny red droplets.

His finger spasmed on the trigger. Misericordia felt the miniature sonic boom of a bullet that ruffled the hair by her ear.

She emptied the magazine as fast as the Smith's action would cycle.

Sgt. Belasco and the security man she'd thrown into him had gotten themselves sorted out and were on their feet. Misericordia let go of the pistol, eeled out from beneath its owner, now deceased. She snapped upright like a gymnast.

The man she'd thrown had a dark bib down the front of his smock, almost obscuring the name TOMOZAKI stenciled across his left breast. He would have been willing to bet any amount of money—Misericordia *knew* this without ever talking to him—he would've bet anything no one could kick his sidearm out of his hand. Especially no woman.

He lost. A roundhouse kick spun the handgun to shatter a light fixture with a serial *pop* of baby vacuums dying.

He surprised her then. He lunged for her, and he was *fast*. He actually managed to grab her and pull her against him, looking to overpower her with his maleness and mass.

She went with him, flowed into him. She seized his mouth with hers and for a brief instant thrust her tongue into his mouth. Then she sideslipped and collapsed his trachea with an oxbow blow of her bent wrist.

He dropped to his knees choking, already turning black. Hands grabbed her around the throat from behind. Belasco had lost his sidearm in the gymnastics. Or maybe he had to crush her barehanded, so he could still be a man.

She reached up and grabbed his wrists. They were thick and furred with black hair like an ape's. She thought that was distasteful, even though he was otherwise kind of cute.

She pulled his hands away from her throat.

"*No way!*" Belasco yelled. "No way a woman has that kind of upper-body strength!"

She pirouetted clockwise, releasing his left wrist. She kept the grip on the right, used the torque of her spin to lock the arm in a hyperextended position.

She popped the elbow joint with a blow of her open palm.

He threw his head back, lips skinning back purple from his teeth, blew out a steam-whistle scream of agony.

"Don't you see?" she asked, smiling her wonderful smile. "I'm not a woman."

She drove the stiffened forefinger of her right hand through his eye into his brain.

"At least not as you understand the term," she told him gently as he fell.

She stood a moment, carefully studying the bodies of her four victims. The one whose windpipe she had crushed was still feebly beating his feet on the parquetry, and the one who had tried to shoot her was still moving enough air through what was left of his lungs to gurgle, but neither was going to be a threat again in this incarnation. She picked up her chair, pulled it back to her place, and sat down.

The man in white pulled the napkin he'd been using as a bib out of his collar. It showed two flawless circles of red. The suit beneath was immaculate.

"You're too much like a cat, Misericordia: you play with your prey. It's dangerous."

"I was made to live dangerously," she repeated, wiping her hands on the hem of the tablecloth.

She looked archly up at him. "I knew it was all a test. You didn't really want them to destroy me. I'm your life's work."

"I kept notes," he said dryly. "What I did once, I can repeat."

She looked at him with something like terror washing all color from behind her freckles.

"But I'm important to you. You know I am. Besides, you said yourself the gene-splicing techniques you used were experimental, that it was a stroke of luck getting something as perfect as me."

He looked at her for a moment, then nodded. "As far as it goes, true. But I have to keep testing you, to make certain you really are what you were meant to be."

She laughed, settled down in the chair and crossed her legs again. "Oh, I am, Dr. James. I'm that and more. *They* weren't so tough. They weren't even smart enough to wear body armor. That's why I played with them some. You can't turn a man into Donovan Steele just by jacking a line into his head and filling him up with phony memories."

"So my lamented colleagues at Project Download discovered. Though Steele himself gave them a reason to stay on-budget—at least until he blew up in Oliver Higgins' smooth ferret face."

She pouted at him. "*He's* the one I want. The ultimate test. Steele."

"It would be more than just a test, dear child. It would be a miracle. Steele's dead."

"But I was created to defeat him. The optimized human versus the cyborg. To prove the machines can't replace us, ever."

She held up her hands. They were clean but for blood congealing around the lunettes of her nails. "With him gone, what good am I? What's left for me?"

Dr. James put back his neat head and laughed.

_10_

"So you didn't really go berserk back in New York, the way the government said?" Jilly asked.

Over on the old State Fairgrounds, six blocks from the abandoned house they were sheltering in, an amplified voice harangued a crowd with words Jilly couldn't make out. There was light over that way, the yellow flicker of bonfires and maybe torches. It could have been anything from a sporting event to a tent revival to a public execution. Maybe it was the Durga Dancers throwing a *kirtan,* though probably they would have heard music if that were the case. Jilly didn't actually care, as long as whoever it was did whatever they were doing over *there*.

The metal head shook. Only highlights cast through the gape of what had been the house's glass rear door by the sullen red remnants of day, sliding on the curve of forehead betrayed the movement to her. He continued to tinker with the strange black polyceram device built into his right arm. She wondered what he used for light.

She had heard of Donovan Steele—who hadn't? The name

hadn't struck her right away, since she had other things to think about than where she might have heard the name of her benefactor. But he'd started telling his story back at the animal clinic, and then she'd placed him.

If the government and media were right, she was in the worst danger of her life, sitting here in a derelict house next to a rogue cyborg who had killed dozens if not hundreds of people. But the way she saw it, if the government and media were right about him, it would be the first time in her young life. She felt no fear of him now.

Then again, maybe she was crazy.

She certainly still felt giddy from exhaustion, despite the hour and a half they'd spent waiting for the firefight north of the freeway to die down, despite two more hours' rest here. Her tongue felt as if it was swollen larger than her mouth from thirst and from having bitten it on her mad roll down the hillside. Her words sounded to her like an unfunny comic doing a turn on retard talk.

Within minutes of the sirens letting go at the Reserve Center, they had heard the heavy chug of what Jilly knew for mortars, and Steele identified as four-deuce 4.2-inch. The explosions had followed fairly quickly, rattling deposits of fine gray ash from the acoustic tiles overhead in the veterinary hospital hallway. Steele told her they were hitting 1700 meters north. She believed him.

There was one more barrage of mortar fire, and after that the firing died down pretty quickly. A little less than an hour later a column rolled south, the vehicles Jilly and Steele had seen roaring out to reinforce plus an extra armored car and two more Hummers. There were a couple of casualties, badly field-bandaged and looking bloodier than they probably had to, stacked in one of the light trucks.

They gave it half an hour for safety and crossed without incident. Within minutes, Jilly found herself stumbling like a wino. Despite her determination—not to give in, especially not to become a burden on Steele—she could barely move her feet in order.

She said nothing, merely led the way, north of the fairgrounds, then across Lomas again into a deceptively normal looking residential area, well-shaded by trees. The neighborhood was abandoned too, lying in a zone disputed by Maynet and Brand. The trees had survived because of the increased rain brought—so scuttlebutt around the Enclave said, anyway—by the outpouring of volcanic gas and ash into the air.

It was Steele who called a halt then, concerned she was just going to keel over. Besides, the Enclave lay near the juncture of the territories claimed, with varying degrees of credibility, by four of the five city councilors, all of whom laid claim to the Enclave itself. With four hostile blocs crowded up against the concertina wire of the perimeter—five, if you counted the Crips, but Mr. Skin disavowed any interest in the Enclave and his gang had never made any moves against the university— the Enclave was best entered at night by a pair of fugitives on foot.

Night had arrived. They were going to have to move soon. Jilly's muscles groaned at the thought of motion.

To put off the inevitable as long as possible, and because she had to know, she said, "Then what happened to you? How'd you wind up . . . like this? I thought they gave you a body that looked just like your old one, after that first ambush."

"They did," shone on the far wall, beside a fireplace filled with the dead ashes of a forager's meal. He'd been getting his lettering down during the lie-ups. Now his laser-light-show writing featured capitals and lowercase and even punctuation. He was able to modify the routines that drove the rangefinding/ holography lasers in his eyes. He didn't like to talk about it, for some reason. "On the outside."

"How do you mean?"

"Well, they rebuilt my features to look like me, and the rest of my body. Aside from my eyes and most of my skin, my organs were intact; my muscles were regrown under electrical stimulus, and everything worked. But it was just for show. Everything important, everything *real*—"

Knuckles rang softly on ribcage. "Was in here. Fusion-driven nysteel."

Jilly shuddered. *If I had messed with that fusion unit . . .* Portable fusion generators were dark secrets that the TV science shows were only allowed to hint at. They were reputed to be absolutely foolproof, of course. But like any good engineer Jilly had learned early that there is nothing in this universe as resourceful as a fool.

Engines fired up to the east. Jilly stiffened, but Steele showed no sign of reaction. She relaxed, trusting his judgment. *Motorcycle engines at the Fairgrounds,* she thought. *Maybe the Weasels are having a rally.*

"So what happened to your rebuilt body? No, well—I'm sorry. I don't mean to be nosy or anything. I just, I—"

"Don't worry about it. I understand. I had to leave New York—you knew that part. I spent some time in Florida, then decided to come out here, to Los Alamos."

"Whoa. Spooky place."

"It's still there?"

Jilly hugged her knees and pushed a joyless laugh through her nose. "All the underground stuff is. The supersecret labs and all that. Rest got wiped away clean. Like Santa Fe. Like my folks."

Something touched her shoulder. She turned her head. Steele had his fingertips there, lightly. The nysteel was cool and hard to her skin.

For some reason she did not pull away.

"Hey. It's all right now." She brushed at her eyes. "Been a while, you know."

After a moment, more words appeared: "I was flying a light aircraft into Albuquerque. It blew up. I remember the explosion, and not much after that. Flash of light, wash of heat— then black."

"I remember, Prophet Buddy's foragers found you all tangled up in the wreck." She paused. Her stomach was echoingly empty, had been reminding her of that almost as insistently as her parched tongue reminded her she needed water. Now she was glad of her hunger, because if there'd been anything in her belly when the memory of that strange ripping sound and the first spray of black-looking blood across the wall and the "robot" and her cheek hit her, it would have all come flying out.

"But if you hadn't heard about Eruption, that must have been at least two years ago!" Jilly exclaimed. "Couldn't you have worked your way out of the wreck? And you didn't seem to be conscious when they brought you in, and how can a computer brain be unconscious—"

The alloy head turned to look at her, ruby sparks dying in the eyes. She felt her cheeks flush hot beneath sunburn. *Being a regular chatterbox, aren't you, kid?* she chided herself.

Steele turned his head back to the wall. "I was unconscious. 'Comatose' might be a better word. As to why, I can't really tell you. The human mind has a tendency to shut down under severe trauma, and my subconscious would have registered the damage to my organic components as massive, life-threatening injury. I had a lot of my own nerve fiber left, and there must have been a lot of pain, though I don't remember it—though I remember the pain of the ambush by Borodini's men in the warehouse all too clearly."

He shook his head. He seemed weary. "Or it may have had something to do with the architecture of my brain, or an undocumented feature of the software they used to pour my memories and personality back in the box they'd built to hold them. I've experienced a lot of that kind of thing, bleed-through from Project Download test subjects, or just the kind of chaos that results when you run any system that complex."

He rubbed his face with his hands. Nysteel on nysteel made a soft ringing sliding sound. "Dev Cooper was helping me straighten all that out. He's dead now. Seems like everyone I know is dead."

Jilly was on her knees facing him. She touched his shoulder. Though cool to the touch, the tough alloy felt . . . *alive* somehow. Yet there was nothing creepy about it. *You've been a techie too long, girl.*

"After the ambush, I still needed sleep, even though my internal life-support system kept fatigue poisons from building up in the organic part of me. Dev said I gave science an ideal opportunity to determine how much of the need for sleep is mental and how much physical. I slept, and I dreamed. Sometimes I dreamed too much . . .

"This was like that. A long sleep. Mostly dreamless. But sometimes—once I remember feeling aware of something *stirring,* something tickling, almost. I opened my eyes and there was a small gray doglike animal, a coyote or a fox, I guess, just raising its muzzle up from beneath my ribcage. It had a loop of intestine hanging from its jaws. I couldn't move to chase it off. It swallowed the loop like a link of sausage, with a little flip of its head, and I blacked out again."

Jilly gasped and turned away. Steele laid a hand on her shoulder. "Sorry," he projected over her shoulder. "I shouldn't have told you that."

"I am not a little girl any more," she said across the tops of her drawn-up knees. She spoke crisply, and seemed to be speaking more to the air than to him. "I have to deal with the world as it is, and the world isn't always a very nice place."

Silence stretched between them. At last she sighed, shook her head, and looked back over her shoulder. "What were you looking for in Los Alamos, anyway? See, I'm OK, I'm back in nosy mode."

He flipped his head up and down, and Jilly had the strangest impression he was laughing.

"My old body back," he said. "All of it."

Before she could find a reply Steele's hand snapped up in a peremptory gesture. His head swung from side to side. He seemed now to be listening intently.

Jilly became aware of the low rumble of engine noise, deeper than the slashing irregular snarl of the motorcycles. The studs of the house vibrated gently in time to it.

"I've been damned careless," Steele wrote on the wall.

And a voice came smashing in through the glassless front window: "THIS IS THE 223D SPECIAL SECURITY GROUP, UNITED STATES AIR FORCE. WE HAVE THE HOUSE SURROUNDED. COME OUT WITH YOUR HANDS ON TOP OF YOUR HEADS."

11

If it wasn't for bad choices. Donovan Steele thought, *I wouldn't have any choice at all.*

Now that he was alerted, sounds sorted themselves out from the motorcycle rally at the Fairgrounds: men moving on foot outside the house, two vehicles—a Hummer light utility truck and an armored car, by their engines—on the street. Other sounds came from the next street over: more men on foot, at least another wheeled APC.

"YOU HAVE TEN SECONDS TO SHOW YOUR-SELVES," the electronically amplified voice declared. "THEN WE HAVE NO CHOICE BUT TO OPEN FIRE."

"Tell them we're coming out," Steele's eyes wrote on the wall.

Jilly stared at him in horror. "You *can't*—"

She started to dart away. He grabbed her wrist. "Tell them."

She twisted, trying to get free. Skin tore on unyielding ny-steel. Blood streamed over Steele's fingers.

"You *bastard*," she moaned. "You don't know what they'll do to me."

"FIVE SECONDS."

"Tell them now."

In infrared mode, Steele's eyes saw tears as dark streaks down the hot yellow blur of her face. She was visibly wrestling with the idea that silence or a scream of defiance followed by a firestorm of gunfire might be the quickest and best way out for her.

"—TWO—ONE—"

"*All right!*" Jilly shrieked. She gave Steele a look of undiluted hatred. "All right. We're coming out now. Don't— don't shoot when you see us."

Steele nodded approval, knowing the girl probably wouldn't register the gesture. She was keeping her head well, under the circumstances.

He opened the front door—strange how hard the civilized reflexes die, he thought; all the windows were long since blown out of the house, anyone who wanted in could climb through any one of them or walk in the back door, and yet he had scrupulously shut the door behind them when they entered.

He urged Jilly out onto the porch ahead of him. Not to shield himself behind her—something Donovan Steele would never have done, even when he was the *real* Steele, in a flesh-and-blood body that was vulnerable to bullets. But he knew the security forces outside would be far less likely to haul back on their triggers in a spasm of panic if the first thing out the door was an attractive teenaged girl than if it was something right out of a Cameron/Hurd technothriller. Even if they were armed with nothing more potent than small arms that would patter off his nysteel skeleton harmlessly as hail, a fusillade wouldn't do Jilly any good at all.

Blue-white light hit the front of the house like a runaway semi.

"So they really are in there," the young lieutenant said, trying not to sound grudging of the stocky officer who stood beside him on the street with his gas mask slung around his bull neck, shielded by the front glácis of the armored car in case the mysterious fugitives answered their demands with gunfire. This was *his* platoon. They were the ones who'd reported the Mt. Zion breakout to Fire Base Charlie—the Army Reserve Center—in the first place. They had been staying alive on these

sun- and ash-swept streets for two years now, and he could
have handled the job without any damn help from above, thank
you very much.

The lieutenant was—had been—regular Army, in Albuquerque with his unit for training in airmobile desert operations
when the volcanoes went off. Eruption had left them under the
thumb of 223d Special Security Group, apparently for good,
if the few and garbled messages from higher up the chain of
command were any indication. It seemed that no element of
the Federal government, civilian or military, had idea one what
to do about disaster-stricken New Mexico. They had problems
of their own.

He had learned early in the course of his brief career that
you got nowhere fast in any man's army by getting crosswise
with brass from base. You got nowhere on the double if the
brass in question was an Air Force Security type who thought
Army legs were lower than dog dirt. But Captain Manning was
an exceptional dickweed, even for a Blue Beret, and that was
hard to work past.

"Bet your dick, son," Manning said out the corner of his
mouth. He said most things out the corner of his mouth. The
lieutenant hated that. "Never much doubt about it."

He nodded his commo helmet, a Kevlar coalscuttle crammed
full of fancy electronics and snugged to his bullet-shaped head,
at a pair of gaunt urchins sitting in the back of the Hummer.
The younger, a boy, sucked his thumb and stared at nothing
in particular with blank black eyes. The other, a girl dressed
in a tattered once-white tee-shirt that came clear to her knees,
clutched the boy's hand and a mutated-looking rag doll and
glared defiantly at the armed and armored men surrounding
them.

"Dink kids," Manning said. *Dink* was base slang for any
indigenous person, not just the Vietnamese who made up a
sizable and uncooperative segment of the population of Brand's
district. "That's the secret. See everything that goes on, snot-
nosed little bastards. Just threaten to shoot their pets, or their
playmates, or their parents, and they'll spit out everything you
want to know. All it takes."

"What if they don't talk anyway?" the lieutenant asked.

Manning laughed, as if the lieutenant was the dumbest GI
in history for asking a question like that. "Shit, Sennett, you

can't let these people get the idea you're *bluffing*. You oughta know that.''

"Here they come," somebody called softly.

The lieutenant crouched, bringing up his compact assault rifle to aim over the car's pointed bow. There was movement on the porch.

"Hit the light," Manning said, very low. He'd switched to command circuit, so that his words weren't blared all over the neighborhood by the megaphone mounted on the armored car.

The spot vomited a million candlepower at the house. A girl stood there, shielding her face with a hand and blinking through heavy black bangs. Beside her—

"Mother of God," Sennett muttered.

Steele had switched to visual mode. Anticipating the spotlight, he hadn't brought up any enhancement. Filters kicked in automatically, stepping down the light input, preventing him from being dazzled.

He stepped forward. Servomotors whirred as the turret traversed to bring its two guns to bear on the pair. The gunner had to depress his weapons as far as they'd go to cover the porch.

Jilly hung back, cringing as if the spotlight were a firehose. Steele kept the fingers of his right hand locked around her wrist.

Soldiers in battle dress were standing up out of firing crouches, staring at him in open-mouthed amazement, in the street and in the yards north and south of the house he and Jilly had sheltered in. Half of them appeared to be Army. The others wore USAF Security Police camo patterns. It didn't surprise him. In the New York City where Steele had grown up, no government agency could hold its head up if it didn't have its own élite assault teams. Even the Sanitation Dept. inspectors who were supposed to make sure you didn't mix cans and glass and paper in one container had cammies and grenade launchers.

There was an open Hummer parked to Steele's right in front of the armored car. He noticed a couple of kids slipping out of the smaller vehicle, unnoticed by the men apparently set to guard them, who were all staring at Steele as if . . . as if he were a walking skeleton of gleaming metal. The kids faded into the shadows between houses on the far side of the street.

Seeing them there, and seeing them get away, made it all easier somehow.

He willed Jilly to stay strong. *After all,* he thought, *these are supposed to be the good guys.*

"Will you take a look at that," Manning muttered—sidelong, of course. "A fuckin' *robot*. Those bozos in that observation post of yours weren't smoking loco weed after all."

Sennett was too startled by the metal man's appearance to take offense. He did notice his men rising from cover to gape. He started to wave them angrily back.

"Come on, get down, you're not a bunch of candy-ass tourists—"

Manning laughed at him. "Give it a rest, Junior. Whatever he is, he cares about the little Mexican twat—and that makes her our hostage. With all this firepower, somebody just *hiccups* and she's confetti."

He stuck a cigar in his face and lit it. "C'mon. Let's go see what we caught."

Jilly glared at Steele through a white-hot curtain of tears. "You *bastard*," she hissed. "Are you hoping they'll let you watch?"

The metal head didn't turn.

Two men in bulky camouflage battle dress came and stood right in front of them. Squinting between her fingers she could tell at once the older, shorter, stockier, white one was in charge. Jilly didn't know too much about body language, but it was pretty clear the black one wasn't too happy about it. Behind them a white kid with jug-handle ears that seemed to be holding up his helmet grinned down at Jilly from the turret of the armored car.

The white officer took a cigar out of his face and blew smoke into Steele's. "So what the *fuck* are you?"

"His name is Donovan Steele," she said dully. "He's a cyborg."

She hated herself at once. *That's what you get for coming from a privileged background. You should know better than to tell the bastards anything.* Even if her benefactor had turned on her, she still wasn't an informer.

The black officer frowned beneath the overhang of his helmet. " 'Cyborg?' I thought that meant 'cybernetic *organism.*' Where's his organic parts?''

"You see too many movies, Sennett. Okay, babe, you step aside from the big fella." He put his cigar back in his mouth and chuckled. "We'll take care of *you* later."

The promise implicit in his words would have horrified Jilly. But she barely heard them. She was staring between the two men at the mottle-painted flank of the armored car behind them. Where no one but she and Steele were facing.

Dancing on the metal in red were the words, "WHEN I KICK YOUR ANKLE, FALL FLAT."

Donovan Steele raised his eyes to the kid in the turret. The boy didn't seem bothered by the fact the muzzles of his paired grenade launcher and .50 caliber were aimed a good six inches above the crest of Steele's alloy skull. The gunner met his eyes as he released Jilly's wrist and began to lift his stiffened right arm, slowly, right out in front of him.

Captain Manning was not a total fool. When he saw the black hole in the center of Steele's palm, he knew exactly what was happening.

It was just too late to do anything about it.

Several things happened at once.

The 10mm pistol built into Donovan Steele's arm cracked. A blue-black hole appeared between Manning's sandy eyebrows, and the back of his skull and about two-thirds of his brain splattered across the side of the Cadillac Gage.

Steele side-kicked Jilly lightly in the ankle. She dropped as if her legs had been cut from beneath her.

The lasers in Steele's eyes flashed ruby. They weren't powerful enough to harm a person, not even strong enough to cause retinal scarring. They were *plenty* strong enough to momentarily flash-blind the turret gunner, filling his eyes with gigantic green after-image blots and filling his head with the terrified conviction his eyes had been burned out. His thumbs contracted on the firing switches.

A burst of 40mm grenades hit the front of the house. Some of them knocked plate-sized sheets of stucco off the wall, a couple went in the front window to punch holes in the interior drywall. None of them went off. It took at least ten meters' free flight before the grenades would arm; the car was too close.

The .50 caliber's bullets went right through the house without slowing down. The house behind it didn't do much for them, either. The burst blew a cloud of powdered stucco off the front of that house and also blew the head off a Blue Beret trotting across the yard.

In case his quarry tried bolting out the back way, Manning had ordered an armored car and a squad into the street behind the target house. A fifty had a chance of busting the light armor of the cars even when it wasn't firing armor-piercing. The bullets were not AP, and they did not penetrate the backup vehicle, but they made a Christ-Almighty racket whanging off the hull and turret front.

The car commander was manning the guns himself. He knew exactly what was happening: *breakout!* He leaned on the firing switches. His car heeled well over to the right as a muzzle flash almost as big as the car itself ripped the night wide open.

On the other street Steele shot the young lieutenant—he wasn't wearing rank badges, but to Steele's eye he was as obviously a lieutenant as he was black—twice with his arm gun. His clip was all silvertip jacketed hollowpoints, not armor piercing, and neither round punched through the heavy ceramic-steel assault vest Sennett was wearing. They did hit with enough force to crack ribs, pop all the air out of him, and momentarily interrupt his heartbeat. Sennett went down in a pile.

Which was the best thing that happened to him all night, because the return fire from the car in the next block arrived then, scything down four of his men as if their body armor were wet toilet paper.

A hammerblow caught Steele under the left shoulderblade and sent him spinning into the side of the car. All around him, what he had reluctantly hoped for was becoming real in roaring ripples of fire, as the men on this side of the house engaged in a furious firefight with an enemy who was their own un-witting buddies in the next block.

He took quick stock of himself. There was a gouge in the metal of his ribcage, but no other damage. A stroke of luck, since a .50 caliber was powerful enough to shatter a joint or his nysteel skull on a good hit. It probably was *not* strong enough to pop his fusion bottle—fortunate not just for him, but for Jilly and indeed anybody within a twenty-thirty meter radius.

There was a side hatch just ahead of the big rear tire. He grabbed the latch, snapped it open, jumped inside. In the right front seat a radioman was screaming into the little insect-leg mike curved in front of his mouth and not making a lot of sense. Next to him the driver was turned around in his seat, trying to aim a service 10 around the turret base at Steele.

Steele plucked the gun from his hand, bent it double, and tossed it back at him. Then he gestured with his thumb: *out*. Driver and radioman popped the top hatches above their seats and shot out of the car like cruise missiles from a sub.

He looked out the door. Jilly was hugging the ground. He was afraid he wouldn't be able to get her attention without a voice, not that she'd have been able to hear him anyway, but she was looking right at him. When he waved her in she launched herself though the open hatch like a crossbow bolt.

"Can you drive this car?" his eyes wrote on the inside of the door as he pulled it shut. A burst of assault rifle fire clattered off the outside as he dogged it tight.

"Who the hell knows? I can *drive*." She lunged for the seat recently vacated by the driver.

Steele slid through the access hatch into the turret.

The gunner had taken his hands away from the controls to devote himself to trying to rub away the big green basketballs floating behind his eyelids. When he felt something tug at the leg of his uniform, he took his hands away to look.

His first reaction was tearful gratitude that he could see. It was quickly superseded as he realized that *what* he could see was a gleaming metal skull leering up at him past his shin.

Like his two fellow crew members before him, he decided to take his chances with the horizontal lead hailstorm outside. Donovan Steele slid in behind the guns in his place.

Military procurement standards weren't exactly something Jilly Romero spent a lot of time thinking about, but as an engineer she had an instinctive, unspoken understanding of the fact that military hardware is designed to be operated by draftees whose ancestors have all been first cousins since the time of James II. Besides, the car was, well, a *car*, not a tracked vehicle or a hovercraft or anything else complicated. The engine was running, and it took her no time at all to figure out how to put it in gear and floor the sucker.

The vision block was small and the street was dark—the strobing muzzle flashes did not give the eye a very coherent picture. There were TV screens set below and to both sides of the block, each showing *something*. But she had no idea in hell which if any of them showed the way ahead. At the corner she cranked the beast left, heading by instinct for the Enclave and relative safety. The car skidded, threatened to roll, jumped the curb, and decapitated a fire hydrant, fortunately long deceased. She fought the wheel, trying to straighten out.

A dark shape turned the corner ahead of her, coming around to face her. In horror she realized it was another car a lot like hers. With the shock of recognition fire bloomed from the other car, unbelievably huge and bright.

Instinctively, Jilly knew the thing to do was *not* to stop and try to back out of the street, or try to turn the car around, in the process going broadside to their opponent. That didn't leave too many options.

She hit the accelerator.

Bracing himself in the one-man turret as Jilly took the corner, Steele saw the other armored car come around from the opposite direction and open fire. He drove the traverse control pedal to the stop, but the turret turned at its own speed, and it was obviously way too slow. The other car had the drop on them and was going to smash them into burning fragments with a burst of high-explosive and armor piercing grenades. Unless—

Jilly charged. The stubby grenade launcher in the enemy car cut loose. The trashcan-shaped projectiles slammed into the front slope right in front of where Jilly sat.

They were too close to arm. They bounced, flew up past Steele with moaning banshee cries as they tumbled.

The left front of Jilly's bow clipped the other car. Her car fishtailed, then scraped past. Steele had already reversed his turret, traversing counterclockwise.

The other gunner was slow. Probably he had paused to watch his salvo take effect and wasted a crucial quarter-second gaping when it had none. Whatever the reason, he still had eighty endless degrees to turn when Steele fired his grenade launcher dead astern.

The enemy car blew apart with a red ethanol flare shot through with the lightning of exploding ammunition.

"BASE ARMORED CAR!" The amplified voice booming out from behind the jetty-jack tank traps of girders and wire that blocked Lomas Boulevard was male, adolescent, and a lot more scared than its owner could have been happy about. "HALT WHERE YOU ARE! WE HAVE ANTITANK WEAPONS TRAINED ON YOU. DO NOT APPROACH ANY NEARER TO THE WIRE."

Obediently the car stopped. Its guns were trained non-threateningly aft. The hatch above the driver's seat opened, and Jilly stuck her head and shoulders out, waving frantically.

"It's me, Jilly! Don't shoot!"

"JILLY." A pause, and then the same voice, unamplified: "Jilly Romero?"

"What other Jilly do you know, Sam? Let us in. There may be bad guys after us."

"Wh—what are you doing with a base armored car, Jilly?"

"Forget the car, Sam. You haven't seen anything yet. *Now open the goddam gate!*"

_12_

The people eating their picnic lunches beneath the elms all stopped talking at the same instant. Steele felt their stares, hot as the ferocious midday sun on his nysteel shoulders, as he walked down the steep hill that led from the law library parking lot.

In fact he could no more feel the sun than their eye pressure, not physically; the only tactile sense that remained to him came from the piezo-electric sensors integrated into his skeleton, backups to the negative-feedback system that prevented him from crushing a child when he picked her up, or a man's hand when he shook. The rest was gone with his flesh, gone with the skin.

Her sneaker soles slapping soft counterpoint to the clicking of Steele's feet on the sidewalk, Janet Virág snorted a laugh through her broken nose. "They don't much like you, do they?"

The Enclave security chief wasn't a woman to pull any punches. Not that she needed to. She was six-two, almost as tall as Steele, and while her build ran to willowy rather than bulky, the play of muscles beneath sun-darkened olive skin argued quick wiry strength, leopard strength. She would still have far less upper-body strength than a man of anywhere near her height, but there was a wildness in her large mahogany eyes that indicated she'd be a savage opponent unarmed on the basis of sheer size and fury.

Not that she seemed the type to get drawn into an unarmed brawl, either. In a scuffed and stained real leather combat rig at her hip she wore precisely the same caseless replica of the old Desert Eagle .44 Magnum that Steele himself once favored, back when there was flesh on his bones. As a combat vet she regarded a sidearm only as a desperation defense, of course. Steele had yet to see her without her 30mm Belgian FN grenade launcher, full-auto capable with a folding stock and twenty-round drum magazine. The only reason she was letting it hang at the full extent of her waist-length Israeli-style sling was that she was tying back her heavy long hair — dark brown, with red-gold highlights in the sun — as they approached the western perimeter of UNM Enclave.

He glanced over at the picnic party on the lawn. Two couples, though their body language suggested they weren't exactly that. One woman was tan and drawn, the other fleshy; the men had moustaches and wore their hair long where it wasn't thin.

''I guess they don't,'' he said.

His voice sounded strange to him. Because it wasn't *his* voice, not yet, though it was evolving that way. Jilly Romero had insisted on fitting him with the speech synthesizer — a shatterproof plastic disk an inch and a half in diameter and half an inch thick, concealed in his lower jaw — before she let herself be led to bed after they made it to whatever safety existed inside the Enclave's wire.

It had not been that cumbersome a process. Steele had figured out for himself that some such arrangement was possible, but assumed that it would involve discovering which neural-interface buses had controlled his speech centers before and making the appropriate microconnections. Cybernetics student that she was, Jilly on the other hand assumed that Steele's builders had designed in a couple of generic input/output ports for direct data transfer, on general principles.

She was right. So it had been a mere matter of hunting up an appropriate synthesizer, jacking it in, and letting the artificial intelligence underlying Steele's consciousness, which handled automatic motor functions when he still had them and generally ran his physical and sensory faculties, deal with figuring out how to make it work.

"These are kinder, gentler kinds of people," Virág said, nodding to the picnickers, who were now carefully looking everywhere except at Steele. "They're trying to build a unified, eco-conscious, back-to-the-land kind of world. They just wanna be New Age farmers.

"They don't like guns and killing. They don't like bad vibes. They don't like capitalism, especially since most of their investments have gone to Hell anyway, what with all the disturbances and Eruption and all. They don't trust technology, except for their blow driers and their notebook comps and their vidplayers. They like government fine when it's signing checks and making naughty businessman behave, and they wish there were a whole lot more. But they don't like *cops*."

"I guess that lets me know where I stand," Steele said wryly.

Virág laughed again. She'd finished tying her hair, picked up the grenade launcher and checked by touch the pop-up indicators that confirmed that its electric initiator was charged, a round was in the spout, and the weapon was on safe.

"Yeah," she said.

They reached the bottom of the short, steep slope. To their right, a dirt road ran between the wire and a ten-or twelve-foot cutbank. At the top of the bank what used to be a golf course was broken up into orchards and organic gardening plots. A pair of joggers in tie-dyed shorts toiled toward them down the dirt road.

"So how are they as farmers?" Steele asked.

"For shit." She jerked her head at the sweat-glazed runners. "If they were really into that, would they have time and energy for that shit? I used to be a farm girl, back before I got big and bad and my mama threw me out. We never felt like running track after we finished working the fields.

"I mean, some of the kids are into it, you know, and they get a pretty good yield on some of their crops. But this place is in the knowledge and information business, like it or not."

The wire was a concertina coil of razor tape along the near edge of the cement flood-control ditch; it wouldn't provide handholds for intruders trying to climb out as wire mesh would.

There was a five-meter wide dead zone, and then a three-meter fence topped with smaller helixes of razor wire. It wasn't wide enough to be an ideal death strip, but the Enclave was working with some pretty severe space constraints.

It would be a good place for mines, of course. Steele saw no signs of the earth having been turned to place them, but of course around here the rain would make the *caliche* flow and then set like cement, hiding mines perfectly. He doubted they were there anyway—too much danger of kids and animals straying in for these kinder, gentler folks. However...

"What do your Aquarian farmers think about *those?*" he asked, pointing his nysteel jaw toward an oil drum welded to a post sunk in cement in the middle of the wire tangle. It was painted bright orange; there were others like it spaced every thirty meters or so north and south along the ditch. They looked like trash cans—except that the posts were angled, aimed about thirty degrees out over the ditch. Small wires led from welded-metal boxes at the base of each drum.

Virág showed him a feral grin. "You know *fougasse*, eh? I guess I'm not surprised."

Each of the drums was half-filled with some kind of fuel mixed with a thickening agent: home-brewed napalm—Steele knew some nasty but easy kitchen-counter recipes from his Strike Force training. The little boxes on the bottoms were bursting charges, command detonated by means of the wires leading from them.

At the press of a button by Janet Virág's blunt-nailed finger, a would-be invader struggling across the broad flood-control ditch would be showered with liquid fire that stuck like herpes and burned like Hell.

"They don't know what they are, *gadjo*. They wouldn't like 'em if they did. They wouldn't like *those* any better." She nodded toward a plastic pipe, spray painted the same khaki color as the earth it sprang from, midway between the *fougasse* barrels. It ran to the lip of the ditch and stopped.

"Gasoline?" he asked.

"Kerosene. It's cheaper, but burns just as hot. The New Agers don't much like me, either, Mr. Man of Steel. They don't have to. It's not my job to be liked. It's my job to make sure they get to keep on playing farmer—or get to keep on doing the medical research that might find a way to reverse the effects of Virus-3, and all the other things Dr. Singh *really* set this place up for—as long as they want. So I try to make sure anybody tries to bust in here dies, and if they die bad enough to discourage the rest of the hot-eyed fuckers out there, so much the better hey?''

Steele said nothing. He gazed out west, past the wire and the ditch and the incongruously jaunty barrels. The land sank away from you here, past Downtown to the river, and then pitched up again to form the West Mesa. A little way north he could see the smoking black of a fresh lava flow. It looked as if it had almost reached the river.

She faced him. "So. You gonna try and take my job, *gadjo?*"

"I didn't come here looking for employment opportunities."

The sound of his name being called made him turn. Jilly Romero stood at the top of the cut above the road, waving. Her hair was tied back, and her long brown legs were bare.

"Steele," she repeated. "Come *on*. Dr. Singh wants to talk to you in the Med Center."

"Right." He started for the hill.

"She's in love with you, you know," Virág told his back.

He stopped and looked back at her. He wished he could smile sarcastically. "In love with *this?*"

He tapped his chest. Metal rang on metal. "You're out of your mind."

Virág laughed at him. "You know," she said, "for an invincible killing machine, you sure don't know much."

In the office of Dr. Jabrandar Singh on the top floor of the University of New Mexico Medical Center, there was little ornamentation and less clutter. The furnishings consisted mainly of a large off-white desk, its rubberized anti-static top bare except for a keyboard and trackball. A servomotor-powered extensor held a tiltable flat-screen monitor anywhere at the command of the operator; at the moment it was discreetly retracted to the side. Three walls were totally bare except for the inevitable assortment of framed diplomas and degrees. Singh's collection was more impressive than most. He was a neurosurgeon, who had been head of surgical instruction at the facility when the volcanoes blew.

The fourth, rear wall of the office was Singh's indulgence.

He stood in front of it now, back to the door as Steele entered with Jilly bouncing behind: a wiry man of middle height in a dark suit tailored with excruciating precision, a red turban wound round his head as if by a machine, his hands behind him. He was scrutinizing a globe of the world, basketball-sized, slowly spinning in space just in front of the wall.

He turned at the sound of their entry. "Our world is a troubled place," he said. His face was dark, bearded, planed like an obsidian spearhead. His voice was high, British-accented with a singsong hint of Punjabi inflection.

"So it has been throughout human history. Yet now we as a species are running out of excuses that it should remain so. Mr. Steele, please sit down."

Steele wished he could still smile. He had no need to sit and knew just how incongruous a picture a metal skeleton made sitting in a chair in an air-conditioned office. But the Enclave chief spoke with the calm directness of a man who expected to be obeyed. Steele sat in one of the surprisingly plain, old-fashioned metal chairs before the desk. It would have been uncomfortable, had he still been capable of physical discomfort.

The sad old world melted into the wall, became a map of Albuquerque in somewhat exaggerated relief, looking like a rumpled blanket someone had smoothed a hand down the middle of. The wall was an intelligent holographic map display, a very fine and very costly instrument. Like the lights and climate control and everything else in the hospital—everything else in the still-settled parts of Albuquerque, in fact—it drew power from the Santo Domingo fusion bottle, which had survived the earth-shocks of Eruption intact.

Singh took his own seat behind his desk. It was the same sort of chair he provided for his visitors. Jilly ignored hers, preferring to hover behind Steele.

Singh inclined his elegant head toward the other person in the room, who sat turned sideways in one of the comfortless chairs. "Mr. Steele, allow me to present Dr. Paul Houska."

Houska nodded. He was a tall, husky man in his late thirties, wearing a black and green soccer shirt and shorts that showed off his muscular thighs. Despite his obvious devotion to aerobic exercise, he was carrying a little extra in the gut and cheeks. His hair was light brown with a bit of curl. A near-handlebar moustache hid his upper lip and made him look like a sensitive New Age bear, or maybe a slimmed-down prairie dog. He didn't stand or offer his hand.

"Dr. Houska was head of the Department of Social Sciences when this was still more university than redoubt," Singh said. "He currently is in charge of our handicrafts program."

Houska dismissed that with a wave of a big hand. "That's not important. What does matter is that I'm the spokesman for the caring elements within our community. Those who are less Western, linear, and goal-oriented than our esteemed director."

It was obviously intended as an ironic jab at the Third World-born physician. It rolled off him like rain off a pitched roof. Houska's moustache twitched. "We are perturbed, to say the least, that you have come among us, *Lieutenant* Steele. Not to mention the manner in which you did so."

"I'm something of a stranger in a strange land, doctor," Steele said. "I came here primarily to return one of your people who had gotten lost, secondarily because I didn't have any other immediate destination in mind."

He sat back in the chair, hiked an arm over the back. It made him *feel* more relaxed. "I don't exactly need much by way of food or shelter these days. I can go elsewhere if I cause trouble."

Jilly gasped. "No!"

Houska flicked her a glance of irritation. "Does she need to be here? She's a *technician*. Also she's *young*."

"Ms. Romero has served me as a technical aide in the past: I find the young refreshingly free of the prejudices which so often lead their elders to misconstrue their own greater experience. Besides which, she is the closest thing we have to an expert on Donovan Steele."

Houska snorted a laugh. "Hardly. Anyone who's bothered to read the whole horrible story from the newsdumps in Zimmerman Library knows more about our distinguished visitor. And his almost unparalleled career of murder."

Steele felt tired. "I haven't murdered anybody. I've taken life in defense of myself and others. Then only."

"That's not what the authorities say." Houska shrugged. "But that's hardly relevant. Killing is always wrong, no matter how you rationalize it. The karma is the same."

Steele looked at him for ten full seconds. "I'm glad you've

had the leisure to feel that way, doctor. You're very fortunate.''

Jilly tried to stifle a giggle, wound up producing something midway between cough and hiccup. Houska glared at her.

"We have a problem, Mr. Steele," Singh said. "The City Council has demanded that we surrender you to them as a fugitive from justice."

"But you can't do that!" Jilly exclaimed. "They'd, they'd—who knows what those bastards would do to him! He hasn't done anything wrong. Laugh if you want to, Dr. Houska, but he saved my life at least twice and freed me from being a slave, and if you want to betray him you can take your baskets and your crummy imitation Indian pots and ran them up your ying-yang!''

"Ms. Romero," Singh said pointedly, "contain yourself. I'd point out that it's unclear the City Council could do anything *to* Mr. Steele. But it's likewise far from clear that they should have the chance. This is why I need to ask you a few questions."

"I won't surrender to your City Council, Doctor Singh," Steele said. "As I said before, I'm perfectly willing to leave the Enclave to take the pressure off."

"Would you shoot your way out, Steele?" Houska asked nastily. "If the caring people of the Enclave formed a living wall around you, would you wade through our blood, as you waded through the blood of so many people in Manhattan?"

"Paul, please," Singh said. "I find New Age machismo every bit as tedious as the older kind. If you and your friends formed a living wall around Mr. Steele, all he'd need to do would be pick you up and toss you out of the way. He needn't bother to wade through your blood."

Houska settled back into sulky silence. Singh looked at Steele.

"By your account, and Ms. Romero's, you were ready enough to fight the Security Police who tried to take you into custody. The Council mentioned that in their bill of particulars. Oddly enough, we've heard nothing yet from Kirtland on the subject, though Colonel Donelson is usually less than inhibited in making his demands and grievances known to us.

"The incident troubles me. The Air Force personnel certainly have a claim on being considered legitimate authorities. You are by training and background a law enforcement officer, and when one scrutinizes those media accounts Dr. Houska presumes I've neglected, it becomes obvious that you have in the past exercised every effort to avoid doing harm to military and police who were performing their duty, even at risk to yourself.''

He leaned forward. "Why did you kill them, Steele?"

"When I was an officer of the New York Police Department, Dr. Singh," Steele said, "the words on my shield said, 'to Serve and Protect.' Ms. Romero overtly feared for her safety if the SPs took custody of her. The patrol that found us was obviously coercing children to serve as guides. That strikes me as the behavior of people other people need to be protected *from*.

"If I've learned one thing in the last several years, doctor, it's that being from the government doesn't automatically make you one of the good guys.''

"Fascist arrogance," Houska said. "Setting your individual judgment above the will of the community."

"I've heard you say those very same words, Dr. Houska," Jilly said sweetly. "The last time the Albuquerque Police Department wanted to search your shops for contraband, just a couple of months ago — remember?''

"Let me make my concern explicit, Mr. Steele," Singh said. "The City Council has no rights over this Enclave which I recognize. It is a collection of petty robber barons whose corruption and viciousness are only exceeded by their ineffectuality. But I am responsible for the safety of our population. Certain people here fear that you are psychotic, a 'rogue' like the cyborg called Stalker whom you yourself destroyed.''

Steele felt a pang his metal face could not mirror. Stalker had once been his best friend, Mick Taylor. Taylor had been caught in the same warehouse ambush as Steele, and like him had been reconstructed by Project Download. But the berserk Stalker had no longer been Taylor. Not really.

And am I still Donovan Steele?

Singh was still speaking: '' —question remains: Was it necessary to employ deadly force? The worst excesses — what Ms. Romero feared, and rightly — seem to be perpetrated by the Security Police. A good number of Army troops were caught at the base by the eruptions, and perforce take part in patrols. Some of the men who died were probably guilty of nothing more than doing their duty, and were possibly under coercion themselves."

"Dr. Singh, 'following orders' hasn't been a viable defense since the middle of the Twentieth Century. You're familiar with the Nuremberg Trails?"

"Naturally," Singh said. "I'm surprised to find you a student of history, Mr. Steele."

"I've studied a lot of things. All part of my job, doctor. I wasn't just a cop, I was Strike Force. We were—are—the best. The élite.

"But to get back to your question—my immediate concern was Ms. Romero's welfare. I saw that as requiring immediate action: If we surrendered the odds were good we would be separated, and she'd be beyond my power to help. I was also concerned for myself, I freely admit. I have no intention of being caged, and the SPs had weapons capable of damaging me."

"So you left the street strewn with bleeding and burning bodies."

"He *didn't*," Jilly insisted. "Most of them shot each other. I saw it."

"They were green troops, and they crossfired each other. I'm not looking to shirk responsibility for their deaths; I was *planning* on them firing each other up. It was a way of improving the odds in a hurry, and creating enough chaos for us to get away."

"Let me put it another way," Singh said. "Do you ever shoot to wound?"

"He had a chance to kill Skip—Hosea Coffin," Jilly said hurriedly. "He let him live."

"Mostly no," Steele said, not looking at her. "I make allowances sometimes. But just because I'm faster and more accurate than a—normal person doesn't mean I'm omnipotent. In most circumstances I'm looking to stop a perpetrator as quickly as possible. A screamer or a drugged criminal—or even a determined one—will keep on attacking in spite of wounds."

"So you take it on yourself to act as judge, jury, and executioner," Houska said.

"I just *act,* doctor, in circumstances where I don't see any other choice. I admit it, I'm not that interested in the welfare of a man in the act of committing a violent crime. And while I'm not real sure about the deterrent effect of capital punishment, I do know that a man I kill when he's threatening a child's life will never threaten the life of that child again."

"I don't necessarily endorse your philosophy, Mr. Steele, but then I am not about policing the thoughts of the inhabitants of the Enclave. I am only interested in guaranteeing that they can live and work unmolested. In my judgment you pose no threat to my people. You may stay. I understand you were speaking with Ms. Virág when my invitation reached you; if you would be willing to advise her in matters of security, that would be greatly appreciated."

"I'll do what I can, doctor. And I'm willing to help defend the Enclave if it comes to that."

Houska leaned forward, face a map of outrage. "He's a *gun*," he said. "I don't know if he's really alive or really just a machine. But all he is a gun, and guns are evil, guns kill, and they have no place here among us."

"If you really feel that way, Paul, you are more than welcome to try to make your own way in the world outside the wire."

Houska recoiled. "It's a jungle out there!"

"Guns help keep the jungle at bay. Mr. Steele will, I think, be a valuable addition to our community. Whether he is appreciated or not."

_13_

"Hey! Yo. There she is."

Turning away from the lunch line with her tray in hand, Jilly Romero made a grim face. She marched to a table by the ceiling-high greenhouse-style east windows without looking back, sat down with a fern brushing her elbow.

"What's the matter with you, Jilly?" her friend Angie asked, sitting down with her back to the windows, which overlooked a sun-flooded terrace and the sort of plaza the university was built around. Her auburn hair was gathered up in a topknot that stuck up from the right side of her head at a forty-five degree angle, like a stag shy a horn. She had a snub-nosed ingenue kind of face, with tilted topaz eyes, but Jilly liked her anyway. Most of the time. "That's Jeff Tillman."

Jilly studied her lunch, which consisted of a whole wheat bun, three green onions, and a container of chocolate milk. "I know."

"So what's the *matter?* He's handsome, he's got great buns, and he's rich."

"He's an asshole."

"What's that got to do with anything? He's got connections *outside*." Angie's parents had died in the Eruption like Jilly's. She regarded the world beyond the Enclave's wire as a dreamland from which unjust fate had exiled her. Tillman senior was a Near Heights construction contractor who was a major crony of City Council member Ross Maynet.

Jilly said nothing. She broke her bun in half. It was cold and slightly stale.

Angie gripped her arm. "Ooh, here he comes."

"Give me strength," Jilly muttered.

"So I hear you're now on Dr. Raghead's personal staff," Jeff Tillman's voice said over her left shoulder. "I guess that makes you too good to talk to your old friends now."

"Oh, I don't know. You never were one of my friends, Jeff."

Tillman laughed. "Well, why deny yourself the experience any longer, babe?"

"I guess I'm just afflicted with taste."

"Hey, she's a pretty stuck-up little techie, ain't she?" asked Beto Hernández. He was one of Tillman's Permanent Floating Toadies, frat rats and jocks who had largely been put out of business by Eruption but still hung on in the Enclave. Tillman always had two of them tagging after him, no more, no less.

"Holy Rollers must've had her out pedaling in the sun too long," said Keith Tauber, the other current hanger-on.

"No," Tillman said, drawing out the word, "you don't understand. I hear crazy old Prophet Coffin has quite a little harem up there on his hilltop. For a man of God he sure likes his pleasures of the flesh. Dr. Singh figures Jilly got some on-the-job training up there among the love slaves that qualifies her to be his *very special* assistant."

Jilly turned around. Tillman loomed right behind her, crowding her space, a tan muscular kid, more lithe than bulked-up, wearing jeans and an old silver letter jacket with a drunken-looking cartoon wolf head embroidered on it in purple. He had light brown bangs hanging in hard hazel eyes. His teeth were perfect.

"You remind me of Reverend Coffin's nephew Buddy," she said, "except he has the excuse that he started out poor. You got to be an asshole amid all the advantages."

Tauber snickered. Tillman froze the laugh in the blond jock's throat with a sidelong look. Then he took Jilly by the chin.

"If you treat me nice, babe," he purred, "I'll forget you said that."

She slapped his hand away.

He stepped back holding his hands out from his sides. "Did you see that? Did everybody see that? She attacked me, without provocation." He looked around at the other lunch-hour diners who busily refused to meet his eyes. "Everybody here's my witness. Romero's cracked under the strain. She's gonna have to go for counseling, get her attitude adjusted."

"Grow up," Jilly said, turning back to her tray.

A heavy hand grabbed her black hair where it was gathered in a ponytail at the nape of her neck. She gasped as her head was pulled back.

"Wrong answer, babe. Now, how about coming along with me for a little *private* attitude adjustment—"

His words broke off in a strangled croak. The hand let go of her hair. Jilly spun in her chair, ready to bolt.

Donovan Steele was holding the youth by the collar. Tillman's blue-striped athletic shoes were flailing ten inches above the scuffed linoleum.

"Put me down!" Tillman squealed, writhing in the grasp. "You motherfucker, my dad'll—*urk!*"

He had finally twisted far enough to get a look at his captor. The color left his face and he sagged.

"I think your pick-up line needs a little work, Junior," the alloy skeleton said. "Why don't you sit down and think about it?"

He swung Tillman toward a vacant chair at a nearby table. The boy hit spraddle-legged. The chair took off along the floor with its wooden legs screeching like a rusty axle on the linoleum. For a moment Tillman rode it, and then a leg buckled and the chair started to rotate, coming apart around him like a jet fighter cracking up on landing. He rode just the wooden seat of the ruined chair through half a widdershins circle, and then it slammed against the wood-paneled divider between food line and dining area, dumping a planter on his head.

Keith Tauber grabbed Steele by the left shoulder, spun him around, and slugged him in the jaw. Tauber had been a starting linebacker back when the university had time for football teams. He was a husky boy.

Steele rocked microscopically back on his heels. Tauber shrieked and fell to his knees, clutching his hand.

"If I'd realized you were really stupid enough to do that," Steele said conversationally, "I'd have blocked the punch."

He turned to Hernández, a fireplug with a broad dark Indian face and a shock of blue-black hair. "Anything you'd like to add to the conversation?" he asked.

"It's cool, man," Hernández said. "Give me five."

Steele complied. Hernández hauled the weeping towheaded Tauber to his feet by the collar and started him rubber-legging for the door.

Steele looked to where Jeff Tillman was trying to extricate himself from the wreckage of planter and chair. A clump of solicitous students surrounded him.

"What on earth is *that*?" Angie asked in a breathless whisper.

"That's Lt. Donovan Steele. A very good friend of mine, and the world's best antidote to sleazy come-ons."

She stood up and slipped an arm through his. "Thanks, Steele. I guess I owe you that tour of the clinic I promised you now, huh?"

Steele nodded politely to Angie and they left, leaving her staring after them with eyes several sizes too large for her head.

In Donovan Steele's experience all hospital corridors were identical. Function defined form, defined environment, from the corridors of Basement Level Three of Federal Plaza, where Project Download had its labs, to the UNM Medical Center. The same anechoic sterility. The same smells. These corridors had stylized pastel desertscapes painted along the walls. They were still the same.

Steele's sense of smell was less acute now that he'd lost his flesh. The folds of the inside of the human nose were an excellent particle trap, and ensured that inhaled air and anything it carried with it would be run past an enormous number of sensors before passing down into the lungs. Even without that advantage his sense of smell was keener than most humans', but, as with his hearing without the enhancement of the echo chambers of his ears, he had lost a bit of the edge he once had. The Med Center corridors smelled of disinfectant and alcohol, but Steele's augmented senses were still sharp enough to strip them away to reveal what those scents masked: the smell of decay, the smell of fear, the smell of death. Every hospital is a charnel house. Steele, who had sent so many men into those white caverns never to return, who had served so much time in that muted sterilized hell, knew that better than most. He didn't need his olfactory sense to remind him.

Jilly was talking in that bright bird-chatter way of a young person with too much on her mind that she doesn't want to say, or doesn't know how to.

"Our most important work is in biotech. We think we're near to perfecting a counter-virus specific to all forms of the Virus." She didn't need to specify *which* virus; it was a given. Steele had lost his parents and siblings to Virus–3, the Screamer phase, years ago when he was young.

"You probably know that on the microscopic level, things like antibodies and viruses work in an essentially mechanical way," she said.

"I've heard that." He nodded politely to a technician with a green smock and her hair in a severe bun. He tried not to be aware of the way she stopped and stared after him.

"The Virus has taken a lot of forms, but to remain human-virulent—to, ah, to attack people—it's got to keep some characteristics in common. We think we've identified several key sequences in the protein coat. That's the way they cured AIDS, you know, back before the end of the Twentieth Century."

He nodded, again being polite. To him AIDS was part of ancient history, one with the Black Death and Typhoid Mary. His own historical interest had never extended to epidemiology.

She turned into an open doorway and led him into a darkened lab. Masses of machinery gleamed mysteriously on either side; ominously, thought Steele, whose exposure to advanced medical technology had not been uniformly pleasant. At the far end of the room two women and a man were studying an image on a big wall screen. *What* they were looking at was anybody's guess; the shapes looked like bread sculptures to Steele's untutored eyes. The researchers didn't look up.

"What we're doing here," Jilly whispered, taking him by the biceps, "is more, ah, more ambitious. We're trying to create a self-replicating assembler, a virus-sized machine capable of reproducing like a living organism. If it's successful, it'll be able to detect and repair the damage done by the Virus on the cellular level.''

He looked at her in surprise. "A cure for Screamers."

Her head bobbed eagerly. "You got it. And for, say, Virus-4, which mimics ALS and multiple sclerosis. Any phase of the Virus."

She led him back out. He was bemused at the way she continued to hold his arm, as if it were a real human arm, warm and pliable, and not a cold metallic skeleton. The researchers never did notice they had been there.

"These two whole floors are devoted to nanotech research," she said.

"I'm surprised you know so much about it. Seems pretty far afield for somebody whose specialty is computers and robotics."

"But don't you see? What they're doing is building *machines*. Robots, like, but the size of *molecules*. It's kind of—what? I guess you could say, the final frontier of engineering. Or at least one of them, until we can get off Earth again in a big way and maybe start terraforming the planets."

He laughed. "Slow down. From molecular machines to remolding whole planets is kind of a big jump. You're in danger of losing me."

She bit her lip and looked at him with big eyes. "You're probably right. I jump around too much, don't I? I was alone a lot as a kid. You probably figured that out. I wound up with kind of an overactive imagination. . . ."

"Hold up. Don't get defensive on me, either. If I have trouble dealing with the scope of your dreams, I don't think that's a lack in you."

She gave him a smile that was simultaneously half-skeptical and half-relieved. "You're sweet. But come on downstairs. I have something to show you that's maybe a little easier to deal with."

14

"This," Dr. Eleanor Ngoya said in her crisp British accent, tapping on glass Steele recognized as shatterproof, "is a forced-growth culturing vessel. Its interior lining is removable, woven of ceramic fiber extruded and processed in vacuum in one of the orbitals. Guaranteed non-reactive and non-allergenic, and free of any organic or inorganic contamination."

Through the window it looked vaguely like an old ice-cream maker Steele had seen in a museum when he was a kid. It was just a matte-white barrel about a meter high with insulated tubing leading into the lid.

"What's it for?" Steele asked.

The Nigerian-born doctor stood peering at the vessel a moment longer, tapping her upper teeth with a light-stylus. Her teeth were startlingly white against her skin, which was a shiny black, darker than almost anybody born in North America could boast of.

"Half a tick," she said absently. She aimed the stylus at a pad on the wall, brushed its photosensitive surface with a couple quick flicks of laser light. Figures glowed to life in red on the glass before her eyes, written by laser, the way Steele had communicated before Jilly fitted him with a speech synthesizer.

"Indeed, indeed. Just what I thought: The AI nutrient monitors are still letting the potassium level get too high. Somebody's going to have to pick it apart, find out why it's doing that. And I'm afraid I'm perfectly useless at such things."

"I can use the CASD the Med Center uses," Jilly said. "That's 'computer-assisted software design.' ''"

"I know what it is, child; I'm not wholly medieval. Would you? You'd be a love. . . . Mr. Steele, you seem thoughtful, though I confess it's hard to tell."

Matrix, he was thinking, *where the hell are you?* He had all but forgotten about his electronic twin. Perhaps the crash had destroyed or deranged some of his memories, or maybe he'd just been preoccupied with events since reawakening. He was going to have to get in touch with the entity—a downloaded simulacrum of his own mind and personality accidentally released by Dev Cooper. *I wonder why he didn't mount some kind of search for me after the crash. Maybe he did, and couldn't track it down. . . .*

"Beg pardon, doctor. I was just thinking I've got a friend who's really into computers." He shrugged. "I don't know how to get in touch with him."

He gestured at the vessel. "So, what is it you're culturing here?"

"In this case, a kidney," Ngoya said. "Helicopter brought in a renal-failure case from Laguna Pueblo."

She sighed and ran her palms once up her face. "I daresay we needn't fare so far afield for patients. Plenty of people in the immediate area find themselves with various of their parts perforated, what with all the fighting going on. But the so-called authorities won't let us get to them to treat them and do all they can to prevent their reaching us. Such a waste."

Steele stood perfectly still. It seemed as if his nysteel bones had turned to ice.

"Given just a microscopic sample of human tissue—and it doesn't matter from what site, as long as the genetic sequences are intact—we can grow any organ *in vitro* in a matter of a couple of days. Skin, eyes, heart—anything."

The room spun around him, a blur of white. For a moment the only thing he could see with clarity was the image of a coyote, its bristly fur wind-rippled and silvered by the fierce mountain sun, chewing as it raised its head and looked around, aware of being no longer alone. The animal tossed its head up, swallowed.

For one of the few times in his life, Donovan Steele turned and ran.

"Merciful heavens," Ngoya said, gaping after him. "I hope it wasn't anything I said."

UNM Medical Center was a sprawl of buildings representing a whole random range of Twentieth Century architectural styles, from cement-and-glass block to post-modern that still bowed to the soulless spirit of the Bauhaus. Donovan Steele stood near the flapping yellow sock of the rooftop helipad of the main block, clutching a guardrail and feeling the hot dry nightwind blow through his bones.

"I have a dream," Janet Virág said by his side. "Or maybe a nightmare. See, I got this place pretty well defended against attack on the ground. You've seen that."

Steele nodded. From here he could see the Lomas Boulevard gate he and Jilly had driven their liberated armored car through, a few hundred meters up a slow hill to the east. Though the City Council was issuing hourly ultimatums demanding the surrender of Donovan Steele, not one sound had been heard from Kirtland. They hadn't even asked for their car back.

Two armed youths were walking across Lomas just inside the barrier. Though there were stationary lookouts posted on a couple of the higher buildings—one was forted up with a pair of electronic binoculars on this roof, a discreet thirty meters away—Virág preferred to keep her people moving. Her dispositions looked professional, and were marked by a distinctly nasty cunning. Her security complement seemed dedicated, if informal in dress and manner. But it was tiny, and while theoretically every resident of the Enclave would take up arms in its defense in case of attack, Steele had to wonder how much use Dr. Houska and his cohorts were really going to be if the hammer fell. Virág had done all that could be done with extremely limited resources. Whether that would be enough remained to be seen.

"But that way—" she pushed her chin east, "you got the old National Guard Armory where the Blue Beret buttstuffers have their fire base. And they got some of those big old four-deuce mortars out there. They have plenty of range to reach out and touch us right here.''

She looked at him, and for a moment it was as if he could see her skull through her olive skin as clearly as she could see his.

''*Fougasse* and wire won't do diddly against those big mortar bombs, they won't do jack. And old Colonel Donelson, he don't like us any better than the City Council does. So every night I sleep expecting to wake up to a whistling scream, and every day I expect to see this place get pounded to pieces in spite of any fucking thing I do.''

''Why hasn't Kirtland moved against you?''

She shrugged. ''They're supposed to be the good guys. You know how far that stretches in the streets. But it's one thing to go taking little kids hostage and gang-raping teeny-boppers when you're out in the field—everybody's in on everything together, so nobody tells no tales, right? But shelling the university—and the only functioning full-size hospital in the whole damn state—that's something else entirely. General Whiteman, the boss out there, he's actually supposed to be a pretty good man. He's just a little *nearsighted*.''

The wind had picked up, rushing past them first this way and then that, like some huge blind animal trying to escape some unknown danger. The volcanoes, perhaps—the night was full of deep rumblings and sounds like vast impacts, and an eerie blue electric-discharge glow played above the horizon, above the open wounds of the lava pits.

Steele heard a footstep behind him. Despite the disturbing night-sounds, he could tell that its owner was young, female, and in good physical shape. *What a lot my artificial senses tell me*, he thought bitterly.

''I hope I didn't embarrass you too badly in there,'' he said, lifting his face into the brimstone-tainted breeze.

''No. Uh—'' He looked back. Jilly stood staring at Janet Virág and chewing her underlip. ''If I—ah—if I'm interrupting anything—''

Virág chuckled, low in her throat. ''Just showing the man the sights.'' She kissed Steele's polymerized metal cheekbone. She didn't have to tip her head far back to do it.

''Later, big guy.'' Hitching unconsciously at the sling of her grenade launcher, she sauntered off toward the stairwell.

"Maybe I should go too," Jilly said.

"Wait. You don't have to run off. Unless that's really what you want to do."

Hesitantly, she moved up to take a place beside him at the rail. From the dorms across Lomas came intermittent sounds of somebody playing guitar and singing, shreds of laughter and conversation.

"I don't know what I did to you today," she said. "Whatever it was, I'm sorry."

He shook his head. It was easy to imagine the sting and taste of sour bile rising in his throat.

"It wasn't anything you did to me. It was what others did to me. That, and bad luck."

She looked at him and shook her head in wordless incomprehension. Tears glittered in her eyes like shards of glass in the moonlight.

"I had a reason for coming to New Mexico," he said. "I had reason to believe that they had the facilities there to give me my body back."

He thought again of his last conversation with Matrix, that lost time ago. His last clear memory before red fire and blackness. Matrix had disparaged the idea. For months, in fact, Steele's electronic twin had spoken more and more of himself withdrawing totally from the external world—the "real" world.

Maybe that was why Steele couldn't get in touch with him.

"The real thing, I'm talking now," Steele said after a pause. "Not just a coating of organs and muscle wrapped around the nysteel skeleton and synthetic brain, but the whole nine yards."

"But that would—wouldn't that mean you were just, uh—"

"Mortal," he said, feeling an ironic smile he couldn't show. "Vulnerable. *Human*."

She stared at him with her head tipped to the side. "You'd give up being invulnerable? Being faster and stronger and more accurate than any human who ever lived?"

"In a New York minute."

"But what happened down in the lab this afternoon?"

"Reminded me of what I'd lost. Because now I've got no

chance of getting back the way I was before, of being real again.''

He was shaking his head, doggedly, repeatedly; he was riding the thin edge of control. He already felt weak and foolish for having broken in front of this girl once today. He wouldn't do so again, whatever it cost. Donovan Steele would play the hand life dealt him, and to hell with self-pity.

''What do you mean?'' Jilly asked.

''Don't you see? Your lab here could put me back about the way I was before the crash in the Sandias—I don't think you could handle the skeletal stuff, and even if you could grow me a new brain, you'd have no way of downloading my personality into it out of this shell.

''But that's academic now, because even the miracle labs at Los Alamos can't do one damn thing for me without a sample of my tissue. And the ants and coyotes and dung beetles finished all that off months ago.''

Jilly's eyes were wide. ''My God! I never thought—''

He shook his head. ''How could you know Dr. Ngoya's little spiel would trip my circuits? I'm still surprised myself at my reaction.''

''No, no, that's not it. It never occurred to me—''

''Lieutenant Steele?''

The voice spoke from the stairwell. Steele turned to see a stocky young woman with short hair and an urban-warfare camo smock worn over jungle-pattern pants.

''Janet said you'd be up here. You'd better come quick. And Jilly—Ms. Romero too. It's really hit the fan downtown!''

15

Miguel "Mike" Aragon slumped in his chair on the dais, more aware of the glare of the lights, the binding and chafing of the straps under his arm, and the furious sulfur smell that still surrounded him in spite of three showers and two changes of clothing than what the man at the podium was saying.

"I think we can all agree," Wilmer "Spud" Laurentian, the heavyset, fiftyish former Special Agent in Charge, Albuquerque, of the Federal Bureau of Alcohol, Drug, Firearm, Pornography, Subversion, and Tobacco Enforcement, who was Dino DiStefano's chief of security and counterintelligence, was saying, "that it's high time we put our petty differences aside and began to work together to bring law and order to this great city of Albuquerque."

By his bad-road voice it seemed clear that old Spud had been known to indulge in at least a couple of the controlled substances on his list, but then it had been a perq from time immemorial for the federal agents assigned to combat what the government called vices to get first crack at the cream of seized contraband before passing it on.

Mechanically Aragon joined in the polite applause that spattered on the gleaming conference table top like wimpy rain. Everybody had been agreed on that since Eruption. The sticking point was, *whose* laws and *whose* orders. *For the Earth Mother's sake,* he thought, *get on with it.*

It had been a beastly day. The latest lava flow had taken out Orilla Lane clear to the river, and Miguel Mike naturally had to put in an appearance at the disaster scene.

He had told the former householders huddled in the next block over—as close as you could get to the flow, which was still deadly hot in spite of its surface having cooled to a black crust—how fortunate they were to still be alive, to be living in a community whose collectivist values would always be there to comfort and shelter them.

The dispossessed had stuck out the Eruption taking place almost in their backyards. They had gotten used to living in houses with the floors stripped to the cement so that the inevitable pounds of black dust could be mopped up each morning, to going everywhere with respirator masks on against the clouds of fume and ash that periodically suffocated their chickens and dogs, to living with the knowledge that at any moment a cloud of seriously toxic gas—or superheated ash, glowing white-hot and flowing like a rapid river—might sweep their way and end their lives in thrashing but brief agony. In the end the volcano had denied them even a quick death. It had simply shit them out of business.

They gave Aragon back blank, disbelieving looks. Looks that would have been hostile if they thought he was worth the trouble. He was still feeling hurt.

"This latest in a series of brutal serial killings," Laurentian was saying, "serves to underscore the crying need for *discipline.*"

Out in the front row of the audience Aragon caught sight of Dameron Crowe, his dwarfish security chief. Crowe had made a cylinder of his right hand and was cranking it up and down in front of his chest. Aragon winced. Crowe wasn't just expressing his opinion of his opposite number's sentiments, he knew. Then again, the disadvantaged weren't always well socialized. And who could blame them? Certainly not a caring man like him.

He sighed. It was time. He stood.

The other council members looked at him with every appearance of surprise. It was usually the hyperkinetic Maynet who disrupted things by bouncing out of his chair to speak. The Councilor for the West Side was known to dislike being a standout nail.

"Mr. Laurentian," he said, "I think we're in danger of making a fundamental mistake here. This isn't a question of discipline. It's a question of *caring*. What kind of a society are we living in, when our indifference and lack of concern can drive someone to express his anger and loneliness and frustration by committing such acts? I think we all have to answer for this, the more so because we tolerate violence towards and exploitation of women in our entertainment media—"

They were standing up out of the crowd, two of them, black-moustached men in sports jackets and shirts with open collars. Aragon's heart crowded up into his throat in terrified anticipation. *At last, it's finally happening. . . .*

"The problem," he made himself say, "is unrestrained individualism."

Flame blossomed.

The impact kicked the next word out of his chest in a gasp. Strangely he heard nothing beyond the desperate wheeze of his breathing. He staggered backward as holes flew open in the front of his shirt, surrounded instantly by fist-sized splotches of red.

He opened his mouth to speak, but no words would come. The Council chamber whirled about him, and then the dais came up and hit him in the back.

"Ladies and gentlemen," Dr. Jabrandar Singh said gravely, "there has been an assassination attempt made against City Council member Miguel Aragon."

"Good," said a voice from the back of the small lecture hall where Singh had called together the various community and departmental leaders who made up the Enclave's informal advisory council. Several heads turned with gasps of outrage.

"Mr. Aragon was shot some forty-five minutes ago by unknown assailants during a City Council meeting," Singh continued unperturbed. He did not act like a man who was perturbed by much, Steele thought. "He has been removed to an unspecified location. His condition is apparently quite critical."

"Wait a minute, doctor," said Cliff Sanders, a graying, heavyset black man who ran the mechanical engineering program. "How's that possible? The Crips keep pretty tight security."

"The would-be assassins escaped in the confusion. However, Ms. Virág surmises they used polymerized ceramic pistols, which do not register on metal detectors. It is not impossible the gunmen made use of accomplices who smuggled the firearms into the chambers in disassembled form, to make them more difficult to detect by means of X-rays or even body searches."

"Guns," a stocky, short-haired woman in a black and green rugby shirt said, and shuddered.

"The forensics are not of our concern," Singh said. "But let me emphasize that so far this has been an *unsuccessful* assassination attempt. That is where we come in. Aragon's people have requested that we provide the Councilor with emergency medical care. More than that, his aides believe that one or possibly more of his fellow council members were behind the shooting. They have, therefore, indicated their intention to normalize relations with the Enclave in defiance of the rest of the Council."

He raised his handsome turbaned head and looked out at them with the fluorescents dancing in his black eyes.

"Ladies and gentlemen, this may be the opportunity we have been waiting for. To ease the tension and danger we have all been living under, and to give the kind of medical care we are capable of to the population of this unfortunate city."

Applause erupted with enough force to drown the rumblings of the distant volcano that vibrated up through the floors and made the light fixtures vibrate with a constant rattle.

"It's a trap," Donovan Steele said.

The applause died. People turned to glare at him where he stood on the carpeted steps to one side of the lecture hall. The anger in their eyes struck him like a blast of hot desert wind. At his side, Jilly edged closer to him.

"How can you say that, you, you *monster?*" cried the woman in the rugby shirt. "We've all been waiting for this, for a chance at peace."

"What's the matter," a thin man with rimless glasses and thinning blond hair sneered, "are you afraid there won't be a place for killing machines like you if peace breaks out?"

"Whatever I am," Steele said quietly, "there'll always be a place for the likes of me. I wish that wasn't true, but it is."

"*It's not here, Steele!*" Dr. Paul Houska stood on the far side of the room, pointing his finger at Steele as if it were a megawatt laser. "I heard about your unprovoked attack on Jeffrey Tillman today. When this calms down I'm calling a town council meeting on you. You're out of here, mister."

"It's a trap," Janet Virág said. "The Council pukes are up to something. They all hate us like poison, and Aragon's no better than the rest of them. You can yell at me too, if you want. Shit, you can throw me out too; *I* sure as hell would've put the hard arm on that jock bastard Tillman if I'd caught him manhandling somebody the way he was Romero."

"We are not here to discuss internal disputes," Singh said crisply. "We are here to address a fundamental issue concerning our relations with the community, and seconds count."

"Chill out, Jan," a young man said. "It's legit. Somebody really did try to take down Aragon. We just caught the flash on Muhammad's Radio."

"Black Muslim pirate station," Jilly murmured to Steele through the ripple of surprised comment that washed across the audience. "Operates from somewhere east of Broadway and south of here. Kinda the interface between Brand's turf and González's. City Council hates 'em, always trying to shut 'em down. No way they'd lie to help the Council scam us."

"Excuse me," said a young light-complected black man from the middle of the audience. He wore glasses and a green smock with a paramedic patch on the shoulder. "What the Enclave does is one thing. But the Med Center's a hospital. We're talking an emergency call here. Leave the politics aside: I'm willing to answer it, and if there's a risk, so what? Nothing's been exactly safe since Eruption."

Virág shrugged, "You got me there, LeRoi—if all we're talking about is a straight emergency call. And even then I'm not happy about risking you and a crew."

The paramedic frowned. "Mr. Baraka is of course right that we cannot deny anyone medical assistance on the basis of disagreeing with their politics," Singh said. His security chief made a face but held her tongue. "Ms. Virág also raises a legitimate issue, however. What response are we to make to this situation, beyond treating it as a strict medical emergency?"

The hall bubbled over with controversy. The stocky woman in the front row rose.

"Ms. Paskoy," Singh said, using the mike clipped discreetly to the lapel of his suitcoat to cut through the tumult. "You have the floor."

The noise died. She paused to moisten thin lips with her tongue. "We've lived in a virtual state of war since Eruption," she said. "I've seen—we've all seen—dozens of our friends and neighbors killed in senseless skirmishing. That doesn't take into account the hundreds if not thousands of lives that have been lost throughout the city. I say, if there's any chance at all of stopping the bloodshed, then we have to take it."

She brushed her short bangs off her forehead, sweat-shiny in the lights. "I'll go myself if I have to. I'll put my own life on the line."

Singh looked at her a long moment. "Eloquently put, Ms. Paskoy. Much as I respect your offer to risk your life to do what you believe is right, I cannot permit that.

"Because it is my responsibility, and my decision, and therefore my risk." He checked his watch. "Mr. Baraka, can you have your ambulance and crew ready to go in five minutes?"

The skinny young paramedic looked surprised, but quickly nodded.

"Very well. You are going to tend to Councilman Aragon. And I'm going with you."

"It's a trap," Janet Virág said doggedly. She was thrusting herself so violently down the emergency center corridor on her long, strong legs that she had to pause every few steps to let the shorter Singh catch up. "It's a set-up, doctor. Every inch of the way."

"Aragon's people are naturally reluctant to broadcast the location of the Councilman," Singh said to Baraka, who was striding on the other side of him. "They'll talk to us using a direct satellite link once we're underway." The EMT nodded.

They reached the ambulance bay with Steele and Jilly right behind them. Baraka's vehicle stood outside the automatic glass doors. Its flashers were dark to avoid cluing watchers that it was about to make a run.

Singh stepped out into the night air, which was warm and slightly muggy. Virág pushed past him and planted herself squarely in his path.

"You can't do this, doctor," she said. Her eyes were blurred with tears, and her voice wavered between anger and pleading. "Too many people are depending on you."

Singh's dark eyes flashed, but before he flared at her he took a deep breath. Then he said calmly, "I think I may have permitted others to go into danger in my stead too often. That was always my excuse, that too many depended on me for me to take risks myself. But ending or even abating this war with the City Council is worth any risk."

He touched her arm. "This is what my people are depending on me to do, Janet."

Baraka had clambered into the ambulance. He stuck his head out the rear door. "We're still having trouble with our satellite link, boss. It's cool for voice communications, but if Councilor Aragon's in real rough shape we're going to need a direct datalink into the Center to have a prayer of keeping him going. That'll take somebody who knows more about computers than me or Dave or Sally."

"I'll go," Jilly said quietly.

"*No!*" Steele and Virág said simultaneously.

Two carryalls, each with half a dozen of Virág's security people inside, pulled up behind the ambulance. It was all Virág dared spare from perimeter duty, even to escort such precious cargo. At that she felt she was stretching her defenses thin.

Jilly looked Steele in the eye. "I'm on my regular rotation as aide to Dr. Singh anyway. I'm part of the Enclave too. I feel like I've got a duty to help in any way I can, if we have a chance to stop the fighting."

"Jilly," Steele said, "you can't—"

"Can't *what*, Mr. Steele? Can't risk my life because I'm a girl?"

His eyes stared at her, but they were seeing his daughter Cory, fleeing the maddened Stalker and being cut down in a fusillade of police bullets. She would be a year or two older than Jilly now. The realization robbed him momentarily of speech.

"You've done your part to save the little girl, Mr. Steele," she said so quietly he had to step up the gain on his audio sensors to pick her words out of the wind. "More than once. It's high time I showed I'm good for something other than being *rescued*."

"A patient is waiting," Dr. Singh said. He climbed into the ambulance. Jilly started after, shot Steele a last look over her shoulder, and disappeared inside.

"Got enough room for me?" Steele asked Virág.

"What, don't you think the Gypsy bitch knows her job?" she yelled. Then she covered her face briefly with her hands.

When she dropped them the wild anger had left her eyes. "I guess it's time to let reality override ego. Plenty of room, dude. Second car, I think we can find you a spare piece—"

A screaming split the sky . . .

16

The center of UNM campus was a cement plaza between the Student Union Building to the north and Zimmermann Library to the south. In the day it tended to be hot and grim despite periodic attempts to soften its outlines by jackhammering holes in the cement and sticking trees in them.

But at night the plaza was a different place. With its two levels and broad steps and ramps it was ideal for skating and skateboarding by starlight and the wan glow of pole lights, if you were young and a bit crazy and had energy left over from the work and study of the day. Both the hardline disciplinarians and the professionally sensitive types wanted to ban nocturnal skating on campus. That made it even better.

Carrie Beth Ryan laughed, pirouetted, and skated away from her boyfriend Ron. Missing his clumsy grab at her, he sat down heavily on the concrete rim of the dry fountain.

She laughed at him. Inside, she was thinking she definitely had to dump him. He was handsome, tall, broad-shouldered and narrow-hipped, with the long, dark, heavy hair of a rock star. All the other young women thought he was a fox.

The fact was, he was none too bright. She was, though she hadn't figured out exactly what to do with it yet. She was an anthropology student without a fixed Enclave job, twenty-two and beautiful, with light brown hair caught up at the moment in a bandanna, tipped jade-green eyes, sculpted features with just enough cheekbone to be exotic—a realization that had come to her as a great relief not a year ago, since she'd spent her adolescence convinced she looked like a pit bull. In her brief red halter-top and cut-off jeans and knee pads, she riveted the attention of every male on the plaza, whether they had dates or not.

The fact was, they all bored her.

"Carrie," Ron called. "Come on back. Take a break."

She smiled at an unsubtle admirer, skated around him, and ignored the noise.

"Damn it, Carrie Beth, I'm telling you—"

That's it, fella. Just keep that tone, you're history here and now, she thought.

The mortar round hit the lip of the fountain eighteen inches from Ron's left hip. It went off with a flashbulb rush of white light. It spattered much of Ron in the general direction of the psych building.

A whining shell fragment hit Carrie Beth just under the right hipbone and laid her leg open to the femur. She went down with arterial blood jetting ten feet from her leg, black under the feeble lights. She was too surprised to scream.

"My God, it's the Reserve Center, they're firing their mortars at us!" Convinced her nightmare was coming true, Janet Virág tried to bolt south across Lomas, to the campus where the echoes of the explosion were still ricocheting between the fronts of buildings like irregularly stacked concrete slabs.

Steele caught her arms. "No. That was way too small to be a four-deuce. It isn't Kirtland doing this."

She showed him teeth. "*Somebody* is shooting a fucking mortar into my perimeter, *gadjo*. You want me to just forget about it?"

Singh stuck his head out the door, staring southeast to where dormitory banks hid the place the round had landed from view.

"We are being warned off," he said. "All the more reason to believe this is legitimate."

"But you can't leave!" his security head exclaimed. "The Enclave is under attack!"

"Then I'm willing to entrust it to your excellent defensive preparations. Come, Ms. Virág, we must move quickly."

She moaned, caught on the cusp of duties. The whistling scream came again. Steele turned his head toward the sound and went immobile.

"You're gonna break my arms, guy," Virág said in a steady voice.

The round landed with a flash that threw angular building shadows out across Lomas. Steele released Virág's biceps.

He glanced at the ambulance. It was already pulling away. "Go with them," he said. "I'll handle this."

Virág signaled to the second car. The driver stuck his head out the window. "Danny, you're staying here to help hold the fort. When I'm gone Lt. Steele is in command. Anyone gives him an ounce of shit, I feed the joker his dick."

"Wait," Steele said. "You don't have to leave them here—"

"If the bad guys are hitting the wire, you're gonna need all the help you can get—even you can cover only so much ground, big guy. And if I'm not the paranoid cunt everyone thinks I am, the less people I take with me, the less get scragged when the hammer comes down. Now, haul ass!"

It was a long block to the gate at the intersection of Girard and Lomas. Another mortar screamed overhead and cracked into the compound several hundred yards away as the driver raced the carryall there with more fishtailing and squealing of tires than necessary, even under the circumstances.

Clashing elbows with Steele in the back of the vehicle, Virág's would-be warriors were kids, with the exception of one grizzled guy who looked to be in his forties, who had a bit of a gut, a cigarette hanging from his lips, and a sweat-stained scarf tied around his forehead. They were dressed in a ragged selection of military castoffs, armed about the same way. The kids all stared at Steele with a mixture of fascination, awe, and terror. The older dude seemed skeptical. He just cradled his bullpup-pattern machinegun between his knees and stared out the window.

Steele tried hard not to see or think as if he were taking

Strike Force trainees to bust their cherries in the hell of Manhattan Midtown without getting too many of them or their
instructors greased. There was some fairly serious firepower
here, and the Enclave defenders were earnest as hell. But bas-
ically he figured a couple of warm bodies from any random
Midtown gang out getting drunk on Saturday night could mop
the streets with this bunch. He just hoped the Albuquerque bad
guys weren't up to those standards.

Of the three kids on watch at the gate two were flattened
behind their assault rifles, trying to get their eyes to grow stalks
so they could peer over the sandbags without exposing themselves. The third had a tripod-mounted spotlight fired up and
was blasting the trees and crumbling façade of the old middle
school across the way with it as if it were a laser death beam.

"Turn that thing off," Steele commanded. "If you think
you see something, turn it back on. Otherwise it just screws
up your night vision and gives your opponents something to
shoot at."

The kid with the hot spot looked inclined to give Steele some
lip—*who are you to be giving orders, the Tin Man?*—and then
the last part of what Steele said struck home. He switched the
light off as the rest of the reinforcements piled out of their
truck.

A muted *crump*, and another whistling scream cut the night's
thin skin like a scalpel. Steele stood perfectly still, skull face
turned to the sound.

The round passed overhead and was never heard from again,
a dud. Steele nodded.

"Open the gate," he said.

The defenders looked at each other. "Janet said you were
gonna help us hold out here," said one of the kids who'd ridden
out with him.

"Yeah," a second said, voice sour with hero-worship turned
suddenly to contempt. "What are you, scared?"

"What's going to hurt . . . that?" whispered a young woman,
who was staring at Steele from her sandbag nest with huge
eyes.

"Nobody's immortal," Steele said. "I'm going out."

"You can't run away!" yelled the kid who'd asked if Steele
was scared, rolling his eyes like a horse in a burning barn.
These kids were dedicated, many of them had lived through

their first firefight and more, but nothing prepared them to face sudden death and dismemberment dropping on their helpless heads from Christ knew what corner of the night.

"What he's gonna do here," the older guy said in a quiet rocky drawl, "shoot them bombs down?"

Another round screamed overhead. This one was close—no more than three hundred meters away, which was practically in their back pockets to kids who'd never suffered shellfire before. Two of them grabbed long-handled hooks from the Tuff Shed guardhouse by the gate and ran to pull the wire tangles out of the road.

"Oh," Steele said, "can somebody lend me a rifle, a couple extra magazines, maybe a few grenades? Looks like I left mine in my other pants."

"There it is," LeRoi Baraka said, clutching the arm of his driver Dave and pointing to the abandoned motel on the right side of Central. On the actual emergency scene, or with patients in the box, LeRoi was as cool a customer as you could find. In transit, he was your basic twitch.

Dave was an EMT, a stocky white guy in his late twenties, who had a blond beard, blond hair that covered most of his forehead in straight bangs, and round wire-rimmed glasses. He looked like a chipmunk.

He pulled away from the crew chief. "I *know*," he said in a fierce whisper, as if City Council gunmen lurking in the derelict fast-food parlors and no-tell motels along Central just east of the river in hopes of following the blacked-out ambulance to Miguel Aragon and finishing their dirty work might hear. "Don't make me wreck this thing."

Jilly sat behind driver Dave, pressing one earpiece of a headset to her right ear because she couldn't stand to have anything clamping her head, no matter how lightweight. The gaunt whisper that had talked them through the no-man's-land north of Downtown and then south to what had once been Albuquerque's main drag was silent. She wasn't sure if the connection was severed or not.

Satlink communications were supposed to be pretty foolproof. Actually, with the spotty maintenance on satellites since the war, they had been cranky all Jilly's life. A problem was *probably* in your set, but it was hard to be sure.

Everybody *used* computers, but not that many people really knew how to get down and dirty in the the guts of the things these days. That was one of the reasons Jilly and the Enclave's other handful of hardware buffs were oversubscribed.

"The Casa Grande motel," Dr. Singh murmured from his seat behind Baraka. "A historic place. The great Richard Feynmann stayed there for a time, after the Second World War."

Actually, the motel—a one-story mock-adobe sprawl—had been torn down and rebuilt several times since then, but the doctor was close. For her part Jilly didn't know who Richard Feynmann was.

With the silent black bulk of the Aquarium, its tanks long since cracked by the shocks of Eruption, looming on the far side of Central, Dave took the first turn into the Casa Grande parking lot.

"First row," Jilly repeated, recalling the instructions the disembodied voice had given. "East side, all the way back in the corner."

"Right," Dave said.

"Okay. Okay," Baraka said. "We're here. We're ready to go."

Jilly glanced at Sally Lanz, the other EMT, a chunky, placid woman with frizzy black hair. She shrugged

"He gets hyper," she said. "He'll be fine."

Dave pulled into the parking space in front of the specified room. The whole motel was black as an old coal mine and showed no signs of life.

"Sure this is the place?" the driver asked.

Jilly shrugged. "What the man said."

LeRoi Baraka levered the passenger door open and jumped out. Seeming disgruntled that the paramedic was preceding him, Dr. Singh permitted Sally Lanz to open the rear door and help him down. Jilly made a face and gathered up her portable satlink unit, which would feed the injured man's vital signs into the Enclave's big system, and followed.

"Oh, Christ," Janet Virág yelped. "Oh, *no!*" It had made her nuts to have the ambulance go ahead of the escort vehicle, but the Romero girl in the ambulance had to talk them in. Now Singh and the rest were piling out of the goddam ambulance without waiting for their security to catch up to them, much less secure the place.

"Hurry up!" she yelled at her own driver. "Move it, move it, move it! Jesus, I don't know how anything gets *done* around here."

The ambulance had taken the last east-facing parking slot. The driver cranked the Bronco into the first space next to it, facing north, so they were right-angled almost tail to tail. She stopped so violently Virág almost bounced her head off the dash. She glared at the woman.

"Out! Out! Out!" team leader Hung was yelling. "Rhino, Tavera, Lujan, take the left. Gomez, Trott, Jefferson, go right."

Then he said, "Hold on," to Janet, who was about to pile out her door, grenade launcher in hand. "Aren't you forgetting something?"

She glared at the ethnic-Chinese Vietnamese noncom. "What?"

He held up a bulky jacket. "Armor vest."

She waved him off. "Nobody else has one."

"You're not expendable. Put it on."

"Aw, Jeez, Hung. They're already going inside. What if there's a trap?"

"Better you are prepared."

"Fiddle with the windage," the skinny man with the bad teeth, straw-colored stubble, and OD rag tied around his head said. He scratched his hairless chest, which was bare beneath his sleeveless denim jacket with the brood logo on the back. "We want to scatter our shots around."

The big man crouched by the mortar showed him teeth in what wasn't a smile, "Lissen at T-bone. Almost like he knows what he's talking about."

The skinny man took a pull from a bottle of Ecuadorian beer. "Blow me, Scroag. I *do* know. I was in heavy weapons in the army. That's why we got this gig."

"Yeah," Scroag said, showing his gold tooth. Modern dentistry being what it was, nobody much got gold teeth these days. Unless they *liked* them. "Yeah, sure. And before that you was a Strike Force commando cop, and after that you was bodyguard to some drug baron from San Juan, and you was so good at that that now you're a broke-dick biker scuffling for spare change in some one-cow town."

Oat Willie was gingerly lifting a round from the case he'd just opened. The box was so old it was made out of metal instead of plastic. He tossed his head to move the strap of his fake aviator cap, which was lying across the bridge of his nose, and giggled.

"I thought we got the job because we was strung out and in town."

"Yeah, well, fuck you, too," T-bone muttered into his beer. He leaned back against the wall of the long-looted house on whose back patio they'd set up the ancient 81mm tube.

"Hey," their lookout, Vago, called down from the flat roof. "Keep it cool, goddam it. DiStefano patrol's gonna come by and hear you dumbfucks farting from the mouth, and that's gonna be it for us."

"Like they ain't gonna hear this fucking mortar," Scroag sneered.

T-bone whinnied a laugh. "That's all you know, you dumb greaseball," he told the sentry. "We got us a free pass. Tonight we can do nooo wrong. Who you think's *payin'* us—"

Something small and round landed on the apron next to the mortar with a ringing *thunk* of metal on cement. "What the fuck?" Oat Willie asked, staring stupidly down between his feet.

Scroag glanced over. "Shit!" he screamed. "*Grenade!*"

He tried to dive away. Oat Willie threw the round he was carrying off into the backyard and pirouetted in the other direction. The HE round, not yet armed, failed to go off.

The grenade didn't.

Real hand grenades don't send people flying like corks out of a bottle. In fact they aren't very powerful. But they can sure screw up people standing right next to them. Oat Willie's left foot blew off. Hundreds of little steel BBs packed around the grenade's explosive core tore through his body and Scroag's. They went down.

At the first impact T-bone had thrown himself face first on the random weeds that had long since replaced the lawn. On the rooftop Vago was screaming louder than Scroag—Oat Willie wasn't making noise, or doing much of anything, in fact—and T-bone glanced up to see the lookout rise up from behind

the parapet, firing his Smith & Wesson riot gun into the backyard as fast as he could jack the slide.

T-bone had his .44 magnum revolver out in front of him in
both tattooed hands. He twisted around, looking frantically over
the sights for whatever was scaring the shit out of Vago.

It came out of the darkness, a horrible skeleton figure that
reflected the shotgun blasts in raw orange chunks, as if it were
made all of metal. Impossibly it held an M-16 at its hip. A
pencil-thin line of red light darted from either eye socket, con-
verging upward. The rifle came up, stuttered a quick burst.
Vago screamed more shrilly than before. T-bone heard a heavy
thud as his body hit the roof.

T-bone let his cylinder go in a bucking orgasm. Every other
round was a steel-jacketed armor-piercer. They sparked as they
glanced off the horror's ribs and skull. The thing came on,
inexorable as a fresh flow from the guts of the distant volcano.

The hammer fell on a spent cartridge. "*Jesus motherloving
Christ, what in God's name* are *you?*" T-bone shrieked. He
jumped up, threw his pistol at the monster, and turned to run.

Something caught him by the back of his colors and slammed
him into the wall of the house. The breath left him in an
explosive sob and he sank to his knees.

Scroag's screams had subsided through moans to a not-quite-
rhythmic gurgle. T-bone heard the scrape of rough stucco on
the back of his denim vest as a skeleton hand grabbed the front
of the garment and hauled him upright.

A death's head regarded him from just beyond the tip of his
nose. "Oh, God, no," he moaned, turning his face aside.
"*Noooo.*"

"Who sent you?" the thing asked in an obviously synthetic
voice.

"No," he whispered.

The skeleton released his vest. It grabbed his right forearm
in both bony hands and broke it with a quick flick of the wrists,
crack.

T-bone vomited.

"Who sent you?"

The hand had him by the vest-front again, supporting him
because his knees wouldn't. The pain was the worst T-bone
had ever felt in his life. It was as if somebody were hammering

spikes up the raw bone ends. But it wasn't the worst thing he'd ever known.

The fear was that.

The skeleton shook him like a naughty puppy. "Why were you shelling the Enclave? Who hired you?"

"Ah, ahh—the cops. The City Council pigs."

The skeleton grabbed his other arm.

"*Nooo!* Mother Mary, please no, I swear, I swear I'm telling you the truth!"

Seemingly reluctant, the monster released the arm unbroken. It let go of his colors. He sank down in a limp piss-squeaking heap.

"It was the cops. Honest to Jesus. We thought they were rousting us. Instead they gave us this mortar and told us to start lobbing 'em into the Enclave at a certain time tonight."

"Why?"

"I—I dunno, man, please don't hurt me again. I think one said . . . something about a diversion."

Donovan Steele froze. Slowly he turned his face to the west.

It was all very well that Dr. Jabrandar Singh was head of the UNM Enclave. But LeRoi Baraka was chief of this crew, and this was his call, and that meant he went through the door first. No matter what the doctor thought.

It was pitch black in the motel room, and it smelled of disuse and mildewed carpets.

"Mr. Aragon?" he asked, hearing Singh's irate breathing in his ear.

The lights came on, so hot and hard he staggered. The room was full of men.

And guns.

"Sorry, son," said the heavyset man in the bulky dark battledress with LAURENTIAN lettered on the breast. "Looks like you screwed the pooch this time."

And he raised a black 9mm semiautomatic and shot Baraka through the head.

_17_

Cursing under her breath, Janet Virág stood by the open door of the carryall and struggled into the vest of Kevlar with ceramic-steel inserts. It was stiff, unwieldy, and battled her as if it were a dwarf and she was trying to get into his skin with him. Her tiny detachment was winging out along the legs of the ''L'' formed by the two blocks of rooms in good order.

She still felt as if everything was slipping beyond her control. She was good at her job, she knew. She had brought her people through innumerable scrapes the last two years, and kept the Enclave safe, and at the cost of few casualties—though any were too many as far as she was concerned. But nothing was breaking right tonight. Singh and the others had already bustled into the motel room without thought for danger. She was acutely aware she should have been first through the door, to secure the premises, or trip an ambush if one was waiting. But she hadn't been given the chance. Hung had dashed in after Baraka, Singh, Jilly, and Driver Dave, so at least they weren't flapping completely in the breeze.

137

Light flashed through the dust-caked curtains of the room rooms. A shot cracked.

With her head and arms barely poked through the holes of the vest, she lunged desperately for the grenade launcher on the carryall's passenger seat. More shots went off inside the motel room.

Two claymore mines, each concealed in a redwood planter and aimed along the fronts of the room blocks, exploded with a roar and an eye-searing white flash. The six young troopers of Virág's security detachment screamed as clouds of steel marbles shredded them into tangles of limbs and loose organs.

Virág felt pain lance through her legs and buttocks. The anti-personnel mines had been emplaced to sweep the walkways, and only the edge of the spreading fan of ball bearings caught her. Otherwise she would have been torn to pieces with her troops.

She came up and around with tears of rage and agony exploding in her eyes and the FN grenade gun in her hands. A figure stood in the darkened long-blown-out window of the room next to the one Singh and the rest had vanished into, firing an automatic weapon from the hip. It all seemed distant to Virág—she couldn't hear the shots, or anything at all, and if any of the rapid-fire bullets were hitting her, she never felt them. The frenzied flashing of the muzzle seemed to have nothing to do with her.

It was hatred, not self-preservation, that triggered her launcher. As always the grenade up the spout was a flechette round. The figure in the window dropped its weapon and made wild losing-balance circles of its arms as the teflon-coated needles burrowed into its chest like a nestful of yellowjackets. It was very funny.

Miraculously the glass in the window of the carryall's open door had not been broken by the claymores. Now it shattered and sprayed Virág's left cheek with stinging plastic dust. She spun.

There were more figures in the window of the room right in front of the carryall, which was bleeding steam from a radiator ruptured by the flying steel balls. They were shooting at her. A fist punched her twice in the ribs, driving the breath out of her as bullets smashed through the thin-gauge metal of the door.

She stuck the launcher around the door and fired full-auto. She was too close for the 30mm grenades to arm. But they were moving fast enough to bulldoze ribs and soft tissue. Two of the figures in the window fell screaming. The third dropped too, probably from prudence.

Motion caught at the corner of Virág's eye. She wheeled, almost toppling from her feet, but bringing her launcher to bear with machine-like precision. Hung was staggering out the door of the motel room. He was unarmed and his head was bare. His black eyes met Virág's. He opened his mouth as if to speak.

All that came out was a gush of blood. He went to his knees, then fell onto his face.

More dark figures were pouring out of the rooms to both sides, punctuating the night with muzzle flames. Virág felt more impacts, to her body or the truck's she didn't know.

She scattered grenades at the attackers. Some went off, others didn't; she couldn't keep track. The world was starting to drift out of focus, no matter how hard she tried to hold her concentration.

Just to the left of the door where Hung lay sprawled in a pool of his own black-looking blood, a passageway led off into blackness. It offered the chance of less permanent blackness than what was closing in on her from all directions.

Gathering all the strength she had ever had, Janet Virág ran for it.

Only about half the emergency lights on the ambulance seemed to still be functional, but to the sleepy Crip guards on duty at the western checkpoint where Central, Copper, and 10th all converged at the point of Robinson Park, it sure looked as if the remaining ones were doing their best to take up the slack.

The guard in the corrugated plastic and two-by-four kiosk hurriedly set down his card-deck-sized MicroMan player, on which he was watching a pornographic video from Brazil, as the ambulance slowed in front of the barrier. The ambulance looked like shit. Its sides were peppered with small holes, like a metal sign on a country road. The paint on the box was blackened and blistered.

The man who leaned out the window wasn't in much better

shape. His face was blackened and his hair was wild and his green EMT smock was torn and drenched in something that looked a whole lot like blood.

"We're from the Enclave," he said, as if everybody in town didn't recognize the ambulance. Nobody else *had* ambulances. "Got jumped . . . down by the river." He spoke like an eighty-year-old man who had just finished running La Luz Trail, a mile up the sheer face of the Sandias. "Back's fulla casualties. Gotta . . . get through."

The guard didn't even hesitate. The Crips were officially neutral in Albuquerque politics. But Mr. Skin was careful to keep that neutrality slanted very carefully in the Enclave's favor. The Crips had frequent need of medical attention, and Skin liked having access to other goods and high-tech services the Enclave offered.

The quickest route from here to UNM was down Central, straight through the heart of the Crips' Downtown holding. The sentry stuck his arm out and made a circling gesture for a couple of gang members lounging inside the wire with assault rifles slung to pull the barrier out of the street.

"Go for it," he told the ambulance driver.

The Crips watched City Council members and their minions like hawks. They paid little attention to the occasional visitor from the Enclave—Dr. Singh wasn't one of the people paying rent to use their own city government buildings. The ambulance's shot-up condition attracted whistles and loud comment from late-night party-goers clumped on the street corners by El Rey Theater, listening to electric *quatro* music floating from the band inside. But no hard-eyed kids with guns hung on the back of the ambulance, and nobody said anything when the vehicle turned left on 6th Street, leaving the straight-shot course to the Enclave.

At Roma the ambulance turned right. To the right was the police department, occupied by a skeleton crew of city cops drawn from the five different districts and maintained mainly as a matter of pride by the Council. The APD complement were the only Council employees permitted firearms: sidearms and shotguns. The police actively resented the fact, guessing correctly that it was a mark of Crip contempt.

On the left was the jail.

The slam was a multistory white structure with vertically serrated walls. This provided for tiny windows opening into the cells at forty-five degree angles to the street, which allowed the inmates some light and a glimpse of the outside world without offering them too much scope to hang clank for the edification of innocent female passersby—and the not-so-innocent too. Before Eruption, by time-honored custom, both sides of Roma Street in front of the jail were lined with low riders filled with pert nasty girls in paint-tight pants, fire-engine lips, and big hair, avid for a glimpse of their Old Man up in the cells—or an eligible lawyer coming out after visiting his client. Whichever.

These days the jail was a quiet kind of place. Few lights showed. No movement was in evidence inside or out as the battered ambulance killed its flashers and slowed in front of it.

The City Councilors kept a few of their prisoners stashed there, according to the same general principles that kept officers on duty at the Main Cop Shop—all except Councilwoman Brand, who sentenced all her malefactors to counseling and community service. When she didn't just order them driven up in the foothills, shot in the back of the head, and left for the coyotes and turkey vultures.

That particular expedient was a big reason the jail didn't get more business. Small-time perpetrators were generally stuck in improvised lockups in their districts to get their minds right, or accorded whatever other treatment their respective Council member fancied. DiStefano, for example, was partial to whipping wrongdoers, which he thought was beneficial for public discipline, and it also boosted sales for concessions, which he controlled—especially when the punishee was young and female.

But the five Council members were caring, dynamic public servants, who had to devote all their time to the public good, and also figuring out how to do their rivals dirt without getting done in turn. So if you provided them a sufficiently painful rectal itch, you just got dead.

Mr. Skin had use of the jail, too, of course—it belonged to him, after all. He understood that he stood as surrogate parent to his mostly youthful gang members. As a former pimp, substance-abuse counselor, and assistant district attorney for Guadalupe County—over to Santa Rosa—he had a far better grasp of the fundamentals of the role than most non-surrogate parents.

So he didn't use the jail much either. His technique was to be an indulgent, easygoing kind of father figure unless you really stepped out of line, in which case you got slapped back into place in a hell of a hurry, with the help of a zealous corps of monitors drawn mostly from younger kids eager to show class and win status in the gang—Mr. Skin could say *Khmer Rouge*. He made you want his approval while making the downside of his disapproval abundantly and immediately clear. Because, unlike your usual parent, he had no particular stake in the continued survival of any of his offspring who carried adolescent rebellion too far, his examples tended to be quite vivid.

The jail was mainly a drunk tank, in other words.

Nobody was paying attention when the ambulance unaccountably stopped, and therefore nobody was paying any attention when the double doors in the back of the box flew open and six men jumped out, wearing black clothes and black ski masks that were definitely out of season. There had been no legal hunting season in the nearby Cibola National Forest for decades, but then there'd never been a season for hunting with machine pistols like the ones the men in black carried, each with a long suppressor screwed to its barrel. So they might have been suspicious, if anybody noticed.

The first people who did notice them were a couple of adolescent Crip monitors sitting in the big empty receiving room with their assault rifles propped against the uncomfortable padded benches, eagerly poring over just-arrived copies of *X-Men #1347*, in which M Squad gets a hold of Rebel and just kicks crap out of her. The six men burst through the doors and stuck the fat suppressors under their noses, which did get their attention.

The jail personnel on duty were city employees. The men in black just nodded to them.

The biggest-bellied of the men in black went back to the front door and waved to the ambulance. The driver and the man who'd sat in the passenger seat, still wearing their bloody EMT smocks, herded four people out the back of the vehicle, two men and two women. Their hands were held behind their backs by nylon restraints, and black hoods covered their heads. The chunkier of the men had a crude blood-soaked bandage wrapped around his right shoulder. He leaned on the others for support as the two men in med-tech garb prodded them up the jail steps, their feet crunching softly in the gray volcanic dust that had settled since nightfall.

"*Stop!*" the electronically amplified voice commanded. Or at least said loudly. Commands didn't come out that quavery. "*You, by the school—hold it right there!*"

The figure kept coming, striding purposefully out of the darkness of Lomas. The young female gate guard punched up her spotlight. A boy crouching beside her ripped off a long panic burst from his M-16.

Bullets sparked on nysteel. Showing no more reaction to the small-caliber impacts than to the blinding light, Donovan Steele came on. He carried the mortar in one hand, the baseplate in the other, dangling sixty-odd kilos of metal like Tonka toys.

"*Cease fire!*" the megaphone voice ordered frantically— and unnecessarily, since the kid gunner had come off the trigger as soon as he'd seen what he was shooting at.

The barrier was drawn aside. Steele strode through. He threw the mortar on the asphalt with a ringing clank.

"How'd you do it, Steele?" the older guy with the MG asked.

"I triangulated their location by the sounds of the firing and the noise the rounds made in flight," Steele said. "I don't have radar, but I do have good ears. Hearing, anyway."

He looked around. His metal face stopped when it came to bear on the kid who'd fired him up. The boy was trying to hide behind the girl with the spot.

"Good shooting, son," he said. "Just keep in mind that you get more hits if you fire in short bursts. And next time, better make *sure* of your target."

"Y-yessir!" the youth blurted.

The kid with the megaphone approached. "We lost contact with the ambulance," he said. "We think they got taken."

Steele stood for a moment. The watching youngsters had the eerie impression that he sighed, even though he lacked the equipment for it.

"I know," he said.

• • •

"Come on, Buster," the small black boy in cut-offs and sleeveless tee-shirt said urgently. "You come on back, now. Your mama whip you if you get all wet."

At ten, Buster, who wore coveralls rolled well up stick-thin legs in an unsuccessful attempt to keep them out of the river, was a year younger than the boy on the bank beside a beaver-gnawed cottonwood stump. Despite the name, Buster was also a girl, black, with pigtails kind of jug-handling out to either side of her head. She waved a homemade three-pronged spear at her companion.

"Don't be silly," she said with great disdain. "Mama knows you can't hunt frogs without getting *wet*."

"Well . . ." The boy thought for a moment. "Well, mind you don't get caught on a snag and drowned. You Mama whip *me*, then."

"Don't be a worry-wart, Humphrey. I'm not going to drown just *wading*."

She started to say more. A mighty thrashing-splashing interrupted her.

Both kids froze. "Did you hear that?" Humphrey asked in a whisper audible for miles.

"Of *course* I heard it."

"You come back here right now, Buster. That weren't no frog."

Not deigning to answer, Buster started wading downstream along the bank, toward where the sound had come from.

"*Buster*," Humphrey insisted, his whisper rising a desperate octave. "You come back. That was a *river monster*."

"Humphrey Hawkins, how can you be such a baby? There *aren't* any river monsters."

A figure reared up from the water beneath the drooping branches of a scrub willow and loomed over Buster, gigantic and dripping. Humphrey uttered a piercing squeal and vanished into the bosque.

Buster stood her ground, spear ready. The figure toppled sideways onto the bank.

"Oh, Humphrey, come back," Buster called. "It isn't a monster. It's a *lady*."

She held up the hand torch she was using to spotlight the frogs and played its beam over the scarcely breathing form of Janet Virág.

18

"You've overstepped yourselves this time," Mr. Skin hissed through lips drawn almost invisibly taut despite a mauve gloss. The words chased each other like gay squirrels among the two tiers of cells surrounding the common room on the jail's top level. The wax fruit piled on his head threatened at any moment to topple to the cement floor.

Spud Laurentian smirked at him from the far end of the pool table. "Get off it, nancy boy. Nobody loves a sore loser."

The Crips gathered at Mr. Skin's medium-height heels growled. Laurentian thrust his fist of a face forward. Behind him half a dozen city police officers in black assault kit shifted, bringing their machine pistols around to not quite point at the gang members.

Only a slight sidewise skitter of the former Federal cop's pale eyes betrayed that he was less than perfectly confident. The cops and security troopers who had pulled off the ambush at the Casa Grande and whisked the captives taken in it right into the Crips' own jail—right under the Crips' own noses— were handpicked. But they were handpicked from among all five Council districts. They weren't all his men, and he was very aware of the fact.

"You've slapped us in the face," Mr. Skin said, speaking each word crisply as though he were biting off celery. "This is in violation of all our agreements. It is intolerable. It's— it's—"

"A *fait accompli,* yoohoo."

Heads turned. Dameron Crowe was making his painful way from the stairwell, throwing the rubber tips of his tubular-metal crutches forward, dragging his almost-useless legs along after them by sheer force of will. "That's—"

"I know what it means!" Mr. Skin snapped.

"—an accomplished fact. I was explaining—" He positioned himself alongside the pool table, midway between the hostile camps. Leaning all his slight weight on his left crutch he reached his right onto the table, pressed the tip of the rack with the tip of the crutch until it snapped upright, then hooked it off the balls and hung it on a peg at the table's side.

"—for the benefit of Coach, here. I'm afraid he has a little problem with any words he's not used to reading in a game plan."

The dwarf moved to the head of the table. Several Crips sidled away, eyeing him suspiciously. He lined up a shot with his crutch and broke.

Laurentian's face was reddening and swelling, as if somebody'd splashed boiling water on it. "Just what makes you think you can talk to me like that, you twisted little monkey?"

A striped ball had dropped in a corner pocket. Crowe gimped around the table, scoping his next shot and shaking his outsize head.

"Because we're all *gung ho,* pulling together, Spudsie. On the same *team.* Keep talking like that, the Jocks for Jesus are going to make you send back your key to the Tom Landry Chapter House."

He shot again with his crutch. A second striped ball sank.

He had backed both Crips and SWAT boys away from the table, and from each other. "We are going to send them back," Mr. Skin said, prodding at his drooping fruit arrangement and glancing furtively over his shoulder to the cell where the hostages from the Enclave were being held. "We've always had good relations with the Enclave."

"Bull-*shit* you're sending 'em back!" Laurentian yelled. "It cost us four good men and boo-koo wounded to take them. You may claim to own the land it's on, you goddamn yellow flit, but we sure as shit got hold of the jail. And nobody's getting them out of here without our say-so unless they're ready to go to the fuckin' *mat*."

Taking that as a threat to their leader and themselves, the Crips bristled and started to bring up their weapons. The cops trained their pieces on them.

In the strained, savage silence Dameron Crowe punched the cueball. It hit the target with a pistol crack and sank it in one bounce off the rail.

"What you have here, Carmen, is an *arrangement*," he said without looking at the Crip leader. "Something that's worked out real sweet for you and your boys and girls. You ready to kick that all to shit over something it's already too late to do anything about?"

Mr. Skin showed him a mouth like a sprung trap and said nothing. Weapons slowly lowered.

A commotion from the stairwell, and the City Council walked in. They still wore what they had been wearing for the Council meeting earlier that evening. DiStefano and Maynet were in suits. DiStefano looked like the head of a successful brokerage firm in a TV ad for the phone company. Maynet had shed his tie. Barbara Brand was dressed as usual, as if she thought she might find England's King Charles IV hanging out down at the Albuquerque lockup. Tom González was got up to look for the treasure of the Sierra Madre in his white linen suit, bolo tie with turquoise-inlay longhorn-head clasp, and sweeping sombrero. As he came through the door he waved clasped hands over his head like a flyweight champ returning in triumph to the old gym down in the barrio.

Miguel "Mike" Aragon had on summerweight charcoal slacks and a pale pink shirt now starched with dried fake blood and holed and charred by the movie stuntman's squib harness he'd worn beneath it. His cheeks were flushed, dark eyes wild, hair and moustache disarrayed. In general he looked like a poster boy for some substance or practice Spud Laurentian used to crusade against.

Crowe finished running the table, pointed to a corner pocket and sank the eight ball with a bang.

"Good *job*, Spud!" DiStefano said, coming over to exchange high-fives with his security chief. Maynet stood glancing quickly from side to side, looking oddly vulnerable and disheveled, like a weasel caught by a spotlight in the middle of a chicken yard with feathers in his mouth.

"Wh-where are they?" he demanded.

Laurentian turned him a patently false grin of jock camaraderie. "Over here, Mr. Councilman. Right over here." He put a hand on Maynet's shoulder and steered him to a cell. The other Council members trooped eagerly after. Dameron Crowe brought up the rear.

Driver Dave had taken a stray round in the shoulder during the ambush. He lay on one of the cots with his head on Sally Lanz's ample lap while Dr. Singh, in shirtsleeves, examined him. Dave's chipmunk face was very pale and sweat beaded his hairline. Jilly Romero sat on the other cot with her knees drawn up and her arms locked around them, trying to keep herself available but out of the way.

Singh looked up, rose, and walked to stand by the barred cell door. He looked fully calm and pulled together, and not a fold of his turban was out of place. "You have captured us by means of treachery of the most extreme sort," he said in a voice that, while quiet, was edged like a scalpel. "What do you intend to do with us?"

"We could try you for t-t-treason!" Ross Maynet screeched, spittle spraying from his lips. Singh drew his head back, fury rising in his eyes. "You tried to secede from the United States. You defied us!"

Dino DiStefano laid a hand on the smaller man's shoulder. "Fortunately, that won't be necessary—*if* you cooperate, that is. You've got to admit, doctor, you and your people have caused us a good deal of trouble by your failure to recognize our legitimate authority."

"What 'legitimate authority?' You are five robber barons, each trying to cover his own back while seeking to plant daggers in those of the rest. I am surprised you were able to put aside your rivalry long enough to cooperate in this villainy. As for legitimacy, the Crips have as strong a claim as you—and I must say I am disappointed to see Mr. Skin taking a hand in this betrayal, after the medical treatment we have tendered his followers."

"I had no knowledge of this, doctor, I swear," Mr. Skin said.

"*Faggot*," Laurentian muttered.

"Don't you want to hear our proposal?" Miguel "Mike" Aragon asked.

Dr. Singh fixed him with a glittering black glare. He wilted into his collar.

"And to think we put ourselves in this position by trying to save your life," the doctor said softly, and turned away.

"Steele," Barbara Brand said in a sudden shrill voice. "Donovan Steele!"

Jilly gasped.

"Donovan Steele, doctor. You're harboring a dangerous Federal fugitive, or had you forgotten? He's one of America's Ten Most Wanted. If we can deliver him, the Federal government will have to recognize our authority. And they'll have to provide us the subsidies we need to get this long-suffering community back on its feet!"

Spots of color glowed on her cheeks, and her eyes blazed with fervor. González murmured, "Right *on*."

"If you had only followed your civic duty and surrendered him when we ordered you to," Brand said, "none of this . . . unpleasantness . . . would have happened. The blood is on your hands!"

"You've got us as *hostages?*" Jilly asked, unbelieving. "You think you can trade us for Steele?"

"The Enclave's policy is under no circumstances to bow to coercion," Dr. Singh said. "That is invariant. We do not negotiate for hostages. We mourn them."

"But you're their leader," Miguel Aragon said, his self-assurance starting to fray visibly. "Surely they'll make an exception in your case."

"I have left written instructions to the contrary, Councilor."

Tom González stuck a thin black cigar beneath his moustache and scratched an old-fashioned wooden match alight with a cracked thumbnail. "But the people you left behind, some of them might not think exactly the same way. You know what I mean?"

"They can't!" Jilly blurted. "They can't just turn him over."

DiStefano laughed. "He's an out-of-control killing machine,

child. You can't tell me some of your gentle New Agers wouldn't be only too happy to have him gone."

"He wouldn't let them," she said in a voice of sullen determination. "He's been through too much already. He won't just walk back into a cage."

"Maybe he'll just walk *away*," Mr. Skin said acerbically. "Have you ever considered that?"

"I know these Donovan Steele types," Spud Laurentian said gruffly. "They're *weak*. Runny at the core. Sure, he's a killer. But he can't let it go if he thinks his friends are at stake. You mark my words. He *cares,* and that's why we're going to nail him."

"Damn lucky for all of us our Federal law enforcement officers don't suffer from vices like *caring*," Dameron Crowe said dryly.

"He'll fight!" Jilly said, suddenly furiously angry with a whole world of smug, big-bellied men. "He'll come after us, wait and see!"

Laurentian laughed. His SWAT men joined him. After a moment, so did Maynet and DiStefano.

"Wait a minute," Mr. Skin said quickly. "If it comes to a fight, you're on you're own. I'm not laying the lives of my boys and girls on the line for this reward you think *you're* going to get for Steele. Forget all about it."

"I wouldn't go shooting from the hip on these policy questions if I were you, Carmen," Dameron Crowe said. "Not without seeing where the rank and file stand, if you catch my drift."

Mr. Skin looked at the dwarf through eyes narrowed to slits. He turned and searched the faces of his Crip escort. Then he sighed and turned back.

"Our turf is sacred," he said in a weary voice. His face had an ashen cast and sagged at the corners of mouth and eyes. "If we're invaded, we will fight."

Spud Laurentian slapped him on the back. "There you go. Now you're talking like a real man!"

19

"Your crimes will not profit you," said Dr. Jabrandar Singh, standing by the bars of his cell.

Dino DiStefano tipped his big fine gray-templed head back and gazed at him from under the camouflaged brim of his cap. The Far Heights Council member was all dressed in cammies today, with a big shiny magnum auto-pistol at his hip.

"You don't strike me as the type to waste your breath, doctor," he said, and smiled his best baby-kissing smile.

"Steele isn't going to let you get away with this," Jilly said from the next cell. On somebody's inspiration—probably that twisted little monster Crowe, though DiStefano was reluctant to acknowledge that he might have anything to offer besides the entertainment value of watching him die—the prisoners had been split up into separate cells, though Lanz was put in with the wounded man, Dave, so she could look after him. It wouldn't do to have any hostages dying too soon.

DiStefano turned and studied her. An attractive girl, he thought. Damned attractive.

"That's exactly what we're counting on, Ms. Romero. You

see, we're not quite naïve enough to believe that Donovan Steele is simply going to allow himself to be led meekly to slaughter. We *assume* he's coming after you. And we're quite ready for him.''

She laughed. He felt his cheeks tighten. She was impertinent, too. *Interesting.*

''He'll wade through your goons,'' she said, her eyes fierce and bright. ''Bullets won't even slow him down.''

''We've done our homework, Ms. Romero. We're quite aware of that. We even realize he might make it all the way here. That's why the preparations.''

He gestured around at the men fixing objects to the bars of the unoccupied cells on both tiers. ''Command detonated explosive devices. Most of them are shaped charges, capable of penetrating the armor of a tank. They crisscross the room quite thoroughly.

''Because the destructive force of shaped charges dissipates quite rapidly in air, and the chance exists that Steele might evade their effects, we are also emplacing a number of charges that will dust white phosphorus over the entire cellblock. White phosphorus burns at a heat of 2700 degrees Centigrade. That's enough to melt even the nysteel alloy your Lieutenant Steele uses for bones. If he actually reaches you here, he will find himself trapped in the midst of an inferno even he can't survive.''

The smile broadened. ''Of course, neither will you. So perhaps you can find it in all of yourselves to root for our brave defenders?''

He waved over a man in jailer's coveralls, who shuffled up and unlocked the door to Jilly's cell. A pair of husky cops with unsnapped holsters came and stood by the door as the Councilor stepped inside.

He approached Jilly. She backed away from him, eying him warily.

''Come, child,'' he said, his baritone deepening, ''don't be scared of me. I'm not a bad man, nor a cruel one. I'm just a public servant whose duty requires him to make tough decisions.''

The backs of her legs hit the cot. She sat down. Before she could react he grabbed her chin and tipped her head back.

''Pretty—so pretty,'' he murmured. ''I had a daughter, you

know. She'd be your age, or maybe a couple of years older.''

He gazed at the narrow slice of blue afternoon sky that the barred window displayed. "She . . . died."

"I'm sure she's much happier now," Jilly said.

His open-hand slap made her brain freewheel in her head. She gasped, had to clutch the cot for balance.

As from far away she heard Dr. Singh's indignant protest, heard Sally Lanz yell, "Leave her alone, you son of a bitch."

DiStefano stood over Jilly, eyes blazing. She tensed to leap for his throat. The cops reached for their sidearms.

The heavy metal door to the stairwell opened. Spud Laurentian stuck his close-cropped head in. "Boss, you better come on. The others are meeting down at Civic Plaza."

DiStefano spun and left the cell. The door clanged shut. It sounded like forever coming down hard.

Miguel "Mike" Aragon smiled and nodded at Tay as his bodyguard opened the door of his limousine for him. He stepped out and stood blinking in the heat and sunlight of the cement desert of Civic Plaza west of the jail. Dwight came up and stood flanking him. Like his fellow bodyguard, Dwight was wearing sports coat and slacks today, just like any other day. They didn't get into the cammie scene. They preferred to think of their role as primarily a *nurturing* one.

Aragon couldn't imagine why their putative boss Dameron Crowe referred to them as "ninnyhammers" and was always trying to get rid of them.

The Councilor was wearing real-person clothes too, in this case a tan suit. He was definitely not the camouflage type either. That put him in the minority today.

The square was writhing with discount-store camouflage. Most of the troops from the five Council districts were wearing them, while the Crips' customary costume ran to variations on black tee-shirts and camo pants anyway.

And every one of the two hundred or so men and women gathered across from the burned-out husk of the convention center was carrying a gun. Sometimes more than one. Aragon shivered. He knew that guns exerted an awful, evil fascination that inevitably caused people to run amok and *use* them. Dwight and Tay had to carry guns, of course. But they didn't *like* them.

He recognized his fellow Council members standing in a

clump and wandered toward them. DiStefano and Maynet were camouflaged head to toe—Maynet's were tiger-striped, and looked as if he'd had them pressed. Barbara Brand wore a pink blouse and a bonnet and a long white skirt, and carried a parasol, and looked as if she'd wandered out of the barbeque in *Gone With the Wind,* but at least it wasn't camouflage. González topped his cammies off with an officer's peaked cap and mirror sunglasses, which made him look like a Third World dictator. The best you could say was that it was a different stereotype for him.

Mr. Skin was there too. He wore plain olive-drab fatigues, without rank or unit badges but with MR. SKIN stenciled over the left breast. An OD rag tied around his hairless head and heavy black liner around the eyes completed the ensemble.

Dameron Crowe leaned on one crutch pointing out troop dispositions on a big map unrolled on the pavement with the other. "Our main force will take up position on Central west of the railroad tracks," he was saying. "According to Mr. Laurentian's projections, that's one of the two most likely avenues of approach."

He looked up then, saw his boss, and smiled crookedly. He raised the crutch he was using as a pointer to his boss in sardonic salute.

"Ave, Caesar imperator! Morituri te salutant. Me, too."

Miguel Mike blinked. Mr. Skin gave the dwarf a look.

Aragon glanced down at the map as if he could read the arcane felt-tip symbols portraying troop and weapons emplacements. It was a standard city street map, a giveaway from a local bank. To tell the truth, he wasn't all that adept at making sense out of it *without* the marks.

"So," he said, "can we actually stop him?"

Everybody looked at him. Maynet's mouth twisted like a rag. "Oh, for *Christ's* sake—"

DiStefano laid a calming hand on Maynet's shoulder. "Well," Aragon said, a defensive whine coming into his voice, "I mean, he *is* supposed to be an invincible killing machine and all."

"Now, Mr. Aragon," Laurentian said, interposing himself smoothly, "you have to understand your modern anti-tank weapons—like your M-91 Light Anti-tank Weapon here."

He bent over, doing a good job hiding the effort it took,

what with his paunch and bulky armor vest, and picked up a polymer tube about ten centimeters thick and maybe two-thirds of a meter long that was holding down one edge of the map. It had a smaller tube fastened to the side of it.

"They're designed to take out armor, right?"

Aragon nodded warily, sure this was a trick question. "Say yes," Crowe murmured out the side of his mouth.

"Yes," Aragon said.

Laurentian bobbed his close-cropped head as if Aragon had just named him beneficiary on his life insurance. "Awright. Our Mr. Steele is pretty much *made* of armor, now, isn't he?"

Miguel Mike could see the point to that. But he stuck out his lip, suddenly feeling mulish. That military-man-forced-to-deal-with-ignorant-civilians condescension of Laurentian's was a bit much for even a compassionate, caring man to take.

"I thought most modern armor was pretty invulnerable to shoulder-fired anti-tank weapons," he said, quoting a half-remembered article in *Time*.

Laurentian nodded, his heavy joviality not even dented. "That's your main battle tank armor—spaced armor, reactive armor, foamed armor, polyceram mesh armor, the whole nine yards. Pretty fancy stuff. Expensive. Bulky, too. Steele doesn't have anything like that, or he'd look like the Michelin Tire Man."

"Look a lot like you, then, huh?" Crowe said. Not loudly, but not quietly either.

Laurentian showed no sign of hearing. "According to the information we received from the Federal government, Steele's skeleton is made up of tubular nysteel. Tough, but not invulnerable. Matter of fact, we got a little demonstration all set up to show the power of these babies."

He turned and tossed the launcher to a Vietnamese in black SWAT battle dress. He uncapped it and extended the telescoping launch tube. Across Third Street several more of Laurentian's men removed a padded blanket that had covered a four-foot square piece of metal leaning against the wall of the Convention Center.

"Now, that's part of the frontal armor of a base APC that got taken out by a mine last year when the Road Weasels motorcycle bunch was in town. Take a look at it if you want. It's a good four inches thick."

Feeling foolish, Aragon trooped across the street with the others to examine the armor plate. It was impressive, he had to admit. It must have weighed at least half a ton.

Everyone went back across the street and stood discreetly to the side while Laurentian's Vietnamese aide put the launcher on his shoulder, aimed carefully through the optical sight attached to it, and fired.

The propellant's whoosh ended almost instantly in a bright flash and a crack so savage it squeezed tears from the corners of Aragon's eyes. He winced, momentarily overcome with terror; he had never heard such a *concentrated* sound.

Everyone else had flinched at the noise too, so nobody made fun of him. They walked back across Third.

The entry hole disappointed Aragon. It was tiny, maybe the size of a quarter. Then a pair of SWAT troopies dropped it on the sidewalk with a ringing clang to show the backside.

The warhead's incandescent jet had cut a perfect cone in the hard, dense metal. Aragon heard himself whistle.

"That's what a 100mm HEAT warhead can do, gentlemen— Miss Brand. We've got over a hundred of these babies, plus fifty or so with regular high-explosive charges, spread out among our units, the City Council, and the Crips. Stack that up with a half-dozen Indonesian recoilless rifles the Freebooters smuggled in through Texas, that pack a lot more punch even than this, and what kind of a chance would you say Mr. Donovan Steele *really* has?"

The Councilors moved purposefully away to see to their troop dispositions. Standing across the street with a grim look on his face, Mr. Skin started to follow.

Dameron Crowe held up his crutch before the Crip leader's thighs. His prepubescent bodyguards snarled and started to raise their weapons. Mr. Skin waved them off with an irritated flutter of his hands.

"Could I talk with you a moment here? Alone?" Crowe asked.

"Yes."

The kid bodyguards looked scandalized. "But, *Jefe*—"

"*Basta!*" Skin snapped. "Enough. He's a crippled dwarf. Do you think I can't take care of myself?"

Muttering, the guards backed off a few meters. Mr. Skin

turned to Crowe. "I apologize for that. Heat of the moment, you know."

Crowe nodded. "No problem. I *am* a crippled goddam dwarf. That bothers other people more than me."

He tipped his head to the side. "You're not too happy with the arrangements, I get the feeling?"

"How can I be? The City Council comes up with a lunatic scheme and then drags me and my Crips into it against my will. Whatever happens, a lot of people are going to die—and *we're* not going to get anything from it but the chance to shed our blood. The worst thing is, I can't keep my people out of it. Crip honor requires us to die defending our turf."

"Yeah. It's a nasty thing, honor. But I tell you what. Your gang's *machismo* insists they gotta take their place on the front lines, right?"

Mr. Skin nodded.

"So the Convention Center parking garage gives you perfect fields of fire down Tijeras and Marquette where they join up at the railroad overpass and turn into Grand. And Grand's right up the goddam middle from UNM. Put your people in there, nobody can ever accuse 'em of cowardice. Stupidity, maybe, but not cowardice." He tipped his big head and laid a finger next to the wart sprouting from his right nostril. "Word to the wise."

Mr. Skin scrutinized the small man with narrow obsidian eyes. It made him look like a blue-tailed racer lizard, Crowe thought.

"You're right," the gang leader said guardedly.

"So if you put them there, I think you'll be happy with the way things turn out. Make the best of a goddam bad lot, anyway?"

"You guarantee this?"

Crowe snorted. "Run back to Mommy, mister. No guarantees in this life. You got my advice. Take it or leave it lie."

Mr. Skin rubbed his chin and stared moodily across at the blasted piece of armor plate. "Do you think they—do you think we'll stop him?"

Dameron Crowe swung away laughing.

20

"We have spoken to Dr. Singh and Jilly—ah, Ms. Romero—
by telephone. LeRoi Baraka is dead. Dave Duncan has been
shot but his condition is stable. The rest are all right."

Standing by the dry fountain, on whose rim clearly showed
some of the blood shed in last night's mortar attack, Donovan
Steele heard the crowd standing in the twilight gathering before
Zimmerman Library gasp in mixed relief and outrage.

A platform had been set up in the middle of the plaza, on
the lower level. A painfully thin youth wearing a security arm-
band and a self-conscious expression stood behind a lectern,
speaking for the benefit of a pair of PVDF-membrane balloon
speakers bobbing in the breeze to his left and right.

"As you probably know, a security team accompanied Dr.
Singh and the others on the call last night. Ms. Virág was
lucky; she was able to shoot her way clear and escape by wading
upriver to the old Nature Center out by the end of Candelaria,
where a couple of kids from the North Valley squatters' farms
found her. She's in pretty bad shape in Intensive Care, but it
looks like she'll pull through.

"The others—" He paused, looked down for a moment, then looked up and said through beginning tears, "The other seven team members—friends of mine, friends of *ours*—died instantly. All trying to help a lousy son of a bitch who'd let himself be shot with *blanks*, just to sucker us in!"

The crowd growled. "Now, Billy," said Dr. Paul Houska from the table behind the lectern. "No need to be so inflammatory. Thank you very much, you did very well. Let's all have a nice hand for Billy—there. Thank you."

Billy was blinking around, confused, as if he had more to say. He didn't get a chance to say it. He was grabbed by the elbow and squired off the dais by none other than Steele's old friend Jeff Tillman.

"We—the leaders of our Enclave community—have been in communication with the City Council during the day," Houska said, his voice echoing softly from the surrounding buildings. "The first thing I can assure you is, no one more regrets the situation than they."

Somebody shouted, "Blowjob!" from back in the crowd. Beefy boys in letter jackets stationed on the edges of the audience began to crane their thick necks ostentatiously, looking for the dissident.

Steele made the R2D2 bird chirp that served him as a sigh these days. He had gotten a hint that this wasn't going to be his day—evening—when Houska turned up chairing this emergency Town Council meeting.

"My friends, please, bear with me. The City Council has apprised me of the terms under which they are willing to return our friends to us, and I must say, speaking in all objectivity, they are quite generous."

"It's Enclave policy not to negotiate with terrorists," Cliff Sanders said. The engineering instructor stood in front of the crowd with his sleeves rolled up and his arms akimbo. He had the sort of voice that carries without apparent effort.

The jock enforcers started to close in on him. Houska gave a minute shake of his head. From the side of the stage Jeff Tillman barked a command. The letter boys stopped.

"These aren't *terrorists*, Cliff," Houska said, all sweet reason. "They're the City Council. The legitimate government of Albuquerque."

"If they're so legitimate, why do they kill our kids and

kidnap the doctor? Not giving in to this kind of pressure's the reason we've kept together so long."

"Yes. But is that necessarily a good thing?"

Sanders stared at him. As if on cue, Anne Paskoy called out, "We've been isolated from the community for too long. Cut off like this, we'll eventually wither and die."

"My thought exactly," Houska said. "Thank you for putting it so well for all of us, Anne.

"Now, let's all hear what the Council is proposing. They are willing to return our revered doctor to us along with the others. More than that, they are willing to acknowledge our independent existence within the city of Albuquerque."

He paused to let the excited buzzing begin to die back. *Recognition!* The prospect of having the two-year siege lifted hit the crowd like a drug.

"All we have to do in exchange is deliver over to them a dangerous Federal fugitive who has been sheltering in our midst. I am speaking of the creature—the nightmare of science without responsibility, I should say—that calls itself Donovan Steele."

All his life Steele had had those dreams in which he found himself walking down the street wondering why everyone is staring at him, then realizes he's buck-ass naked. Now he felt that same awful sinking as every head turned to stare at him. And this time he wasn't even wearing his *skin*.

"As befits a machine created by the CIA with one mission in mind—to kill—Donovan Steele has caused nothing but strife since arriving. He killed and mutilated several people in a religious community in the foothills, and subsequently caused the deaths of a number of soldiers. He performed a completely unprovoked attack on our own Jeff Tillman—everybody knows our Jeff, let's have a big hand for him now. Mortars were fired onto our campus, tearing apart five of us and wounding fifteen more. And the presence of the threat posed by this Steele, an out-of-control killer with God knows what terrible capabilities, so unnerved the City Council that they put together a desperate plan to apprehend him—a plan which, had it not been for the overreaction of certain Enclave security personnel, would have gone off without the shedding of a drop of blood. Blood which now likewise stains Steele's metal claws!"

The crowd was seething now, like a swarm of bees in a

busted-open hive. Billy from security was being held back by a couple of Tillman's buddies as he yelled something at Houska in a white-faced fury.

"So I submit to you—to the democratic process by which the organism that is the university can make its collective will known—this question: Do we throw away more lives uselessly, following the tenets of mindless medieval *machismo*? Or do we do our duty, to the city and to ourselves, and rid ourselves of this menace which threatens each and every one of us by turning Donovan Steele over to the justice which awaits him? I call now for a vote—"

"Wait."

One word, spoken at the maximum volume the speech synthesizer Jilly had fitted him with was capable of. The faces turned to him again.

"Save yourselves the effort," he said. "I don't care what the outcome is. I'm not surrendering."

"You'd oppose your will to that of the *community?*" Anne Paskoy screeched. "You'd let your own selfishness endanger the hostages and all of us?"

"If it was that simple I might turn myself over. But it isn't. In a hostage situation the hostage takers usually keep upping their demands when the first ones are met, unless they're under very heavy pressure—pressure which we're in no position to bring to bear."

"I won't listen!" Paskoy shouted, holding her hands over her ears. "I won't hear this reactionary garbage."

"Wait, wait," Cliff Sanders was yelling, "listen to the man! We all know the damn Council have all been at each others' throats since Eruption. How can we trust them? It only takes one changing his mind to queer the whole damn deal!"

A roar of anger drowned him out. The crowd did not want to hear that their just-raised hopes of détente with the Council might vanish like a penny tossed in lava. Steele was an outsider. Steele was *different*.

Steele was guilty.

"What are you going to do, Steele?" Houska's voice, amplified through piezoelectric-sensitive balloons made of a substance that was first cousin to Saran Wrap, challenged him over the rising, confused din. "How will you stop us from turning you over to the Council? Are you going to kill us all, Steele?

Slaughter hundreds of unarmed innocents like the mad monster you are?''

"No," Steele said. "I'm just going to ignore you."

He started walking.

The crowd parted before him, sullen but stunned. Suddenly the stocky short-haired Anne Paskoy was standing square in front of him, pounding on his bare ribs with her fists.

"Monster!" she screamed, spittle spraying his ribcage. "*Monster!*"

He kept walking. His chest bumped into her, moved her gently but irresistibly from his path like an icebreaker shoving aside a tiny floe. A gap opened in the crowd ahead as if in response.

"*You saw it! You saw him attack me!*" Paskoy's shriek soared like a hawk from behind him. "For the love of our community and Mother Earth, *stop him!*"

A glob of spit and snot hit Steele on the right cheekbone. The crowd closed in again, jostling, yelling, fists flailing.

Steele walked. He did not strike back, did not even resist. He simply moved unstoppably through the howling mob. He had no flesh for their collective fists to bruise. He didn't let himself hear their words.

Houska's voice rang from the floating speakers behind him. "You're condemning them to death, Steele! You're killing Singh and your little friend Romero!" The sociologist-turned-craft-guildsman was unable to keep a certain satisfaction from his voice.

At first the mob followed him. He even felt a few small objects rattle off his shoulderblades—what they were throwing he had no clue, since there weren't many rocks on the paved plaza or around the duck pond to the west. As he continued, though, they quickly fell away, so that by the time he came around the Maxwell Museum of Anthropology—its WPA phony-Pueblo architecture less harsh and overbearing than most of the buildings on the central plaza—it had thinned to twenty or thirty die-hards.

Most of them stopped when they saw the security kids at the gate. They had been reinforced to a full dozen and were well armed. They had a couple of machineguns and a couple of rocket launchers. The way they looked at the mob was not pleasant.

Their leader was a big heavy-necked boy who looked as if he might have been a defector from Tillman's bunch. He had a shock of black hair falling almost in his angry hazel eyes. He carried a Japanese assault rifle, an SCK caseless 4mm with a fifty-round box behind the pistol grip, compact and lethal. He put himself squarely in Steele's path.

"You're going after them?" he demanded.

"Yes."

The boy held out the weapon. "Here. You might need this."

Steele took it, along with a ripstop pouch of extra magazines. "Thanks." He glanced around, saw a square young woman who looked like a Pueblo Indian with a slung rocket-launcher tube, some Pacific Rim equivalent of the American M-91.

"That HE or anti-tank?" he asked.

"High explosive."

"Lend it to me?"

She bit her lip. It was an honor to be entrusted with so much firepower. Also, she hated to miss the chance to lay some *serious* hurt on the Council bastards if the attack everyone in Security expected materialized.

She unslung the launcher and held it out. "Here," she said, shyly looking at the ground.

"Thank you," Steele said. He slung it, checked the LCD display, made sure it was set to non-illuminated mode, and that the weapon's magazine was full, the batteries for its electronic initiator fully charged.

The security kids opened the gate. Steele walked through. He crossed the six deserted lanes of University and started down Grand without a backward look.

A shout stopped him. "*Steele!*" It was Houska's voice.

He turned. Houska stood in the open gate with his blow-dried hair all awry.

"You can't do this! You can't just go marching in there!"

"It's what the City Council expects, doctor."

"You'll kill the hostages."

"They may already be dead. The Council never intends to give them back one way or another. You'll get to be head of the Enclave, doctor, won't you?"

"Dammit, *what if this makes them attack us?*"

"If that's what they had in mind, that's what they would've done. They don't think they're strong enough, even acting together—or, more likely, they know their alliance would break down if they tried."

A thought struck him, and he looked closely at the man. "You're afraid I'll succeed, is that it, doctor?" He laughed. "Thanks for the vote of confidence." He turned and walked on down the middle of Grand.

Dr. Paul Houska looked wildly from side to side. This was all getting out of hand; he hadn't planned for things to go this way at all.

A skinny boy stood in the open gate with an anti-tank rocket launcher hanging from a sling around his neck. In anticipation of a Council thrust he had it already prepped, a breach of safety procedure that Virág would have reamed him a new asshole for.

Houska gave him an open-hand slap on the side of the head, stunning him for the moment it took to yank the launcher away. The sociologist held it to his shoulder, peered through the optical sight.

It was near dark, but the light-enhancing capabilities of the launcher's cheap chip were good enough to show him a noon-clear picture of Steele's back, fifty yards away. A green box appeared around his image, showing that the rocket was targeted.

Houska sensed people diving at him from all sides. He grinned wolfishly beneath his moustache and pressed the button.

"*Steele!*" A new cry from behind, a different voice, shriller. A note of urgency made him bring the SCK up from the hip as he spun.

He saw a gout of white smoke. He'd seen enough rocket launchers fired in Manhattan's no-man's-land combat zones to know what that meant.

Whether it was a lightning reaction of the Steele personality or the AI routines that helped run his cyborged body he never knew. But his instantaneous reaction was to start scanning his eye-mounted lasers at ultra-high speed, so they defined a two-meter square midway between him and Houska.

Shaped-charge warheads don't depend on speed for effect. They do depend on *stand-off*, the distance between the shaped explosive and the surface it's supposed to damage. If it is too near or too far when it detonates, the blast does not focus properly and the effect is diminished. An impact sensor at the tip of a hollow nose cone sets the charge off at the proper stand-off distance. If the rocket moved too fast, the cone would have to be too long to be fired from a shoulder launcher.

So Houska's HEAT rocket was moving relatively slowly when it crossed the zone covered by Steele's sighting lasers. It was Steele's only edge.

It was his only chance.

His finger tightened automatically on the trigger. Proper automatic-weapons practice calls for them to be fired in short deliberate bursts. He had no time for that: He let it all go at once like a string of firecrackers, moving the weapon in a tight figure-eight.

Time slowed.

A flower of fire unfolded its petals in Steele's face, so quickly that his vision began to overload, blurring into big black and white blocks before his computer-driven filters kicked in. It became a blazing tendril, reaching for him. Steele braced for the lance of incandescent metal. He wondered if he would feel anything.

The tentacle of glowing gas spiked almost to the center of Steele's chest. Then it faded, dissipated. A spray of copper drops struck him on the sternum and face.

The metal was still hot enough to burn flesh. It wasn't hot enough to leave a mark on nysteel.

Back at the gate Dr. Paul Houska was struggling in the grip of so many security kids they were getting in each other's way. The commander had a chunky 10mm out and was trying to stick it in the writhing doctor's ear, obviously intent on blowing his head off.

"Wait!" Steele called. "Let him go."

Everybody stared at him.

"There's going to be more than enough killing tonight. And there was no harm done."

He looked down at the shiny reddish circles spattered across him, brushed at them with his hand. They fell away, tinkling on the cracked asphalt like tin snowflakes.

One by one the kids took their hands off Houska and stepped away. Steele turned and once more started walking toward Downtown and the final confrontation.

21

Spud Laurentian lowered the pocket phone from his ear and smiled. It made his face look like a happy fist.

"He's on his way," he announced to his boss and the other Council members, gathered near a huge bonfire the Crips had built in the middle of Civic Plaza. "Right down Grand. Just like we thought."

Dino DiStefano settled his Kevlar coal-scuttle helmet on his head and cinched the strap under a manfully jutted chin. "Let's go," he said.

As soon as it departed University Boulevard, Grand S-curved tightly right and then left, into a straight shot down a steep hill west toward I-25, the railroad tracks, and Downtown. What that meant was that within a hundred meters Donovan Steele was completely lost to view for the bemused Dr. Paul Houska and his captors.

He was also to all intents lost to view from Downtown, screened by the highway overpass and the high bridge where

Grand forked and arced over the rail yards into the city center—
and Crip stronghold—proper.

The pyramid-capped Hyatt Regency on the near side of
Downtown, which had dominated the Albuquerque skyline
since the last decade of the Twentieth Century, commanded a
view of Grand as it did most of the Enclave—and in fact much
of Albuquerque. Mr. Skin's personal quarters were reputed to
be in the penthouse, up in the pyramid itself. Rumor had them
maxed-out on decadence, with fountains of perfumed water
and well stocked with gorgeous and scantily clad young
women—and men—of various colors and infinite pliability.
Since other rumors insisted that the Crip leader led a thoroughly
ascetic life, aside from the cross-dressing, Steele had his
doubts.

What was important was that, even if Mr. Skin was up there
in his putatively plush aerie, even if he had the whole City
Council up there in his inner sanctum watching the show
through a telescope—or, conceivably, by computer-enhanced
low-light TV—they still were not going to have a great view.
The area between the Enclave's border on University and
Downtown was another no-man's-land, largely deserted—as a
matter of fact every place Steele had been in Albuquerque so
far fit that description, except the Enclave itself. The streetlights
had long since been shot out by rubble-runners and other two-
legged vermin. Even with computer enhancement, the range
was too long to see much in this dark. And even infrared scopes
would be small help, since Steele had been outside long enough
that his nysteel skeleton had warmed to the same temperature
as the somewhat muggy night air.

To be sure, he walked boldly down the middle of Grand—
High Noon after dark—until a crackerbox stucco apartment
block shouldered in between him and the Regency tower. Then
he darted right, losing himself among the trees on the north
side of the street.

Li'l Man jumped up and pointed west into darkness that
wasn't much diluted by a scummy purple-gray twilight band
clinging to the cinder cones on the horizon. "Say man, did
you see that? Something moved down the street."

Tino peered at him with red eyes and let smoke drool out
his mouth. "Hey, mellow out, dude. You just flashing para-

noia.'' He let his head fall back against the stack of old tires out in front of an abandoned tire store which, by ancient tradition, was painted a lurid yellow that two years of desert sun, dust, and volcanic ash had done little to fade.

The northern boundary of Downtown, and sacred Crip turf, was Lomas Boulevard. The perimeter was just strands of barbed wire strung along the south side of the street. It wasn't a particularly formidable barrier, and the strands were always breaking.

Mr. Skin liked it that way. The frequent breakage was a ready source of small, easily completed tasks to keep his teen warriors occupied. The relatively fragile nature of the perimeter was a clear message to the City Council as to just how seriously he took the threat they posed to him.

Of course a major source of breakage was derelicts and would-be thieves cutting the wire. They were always being strung up at various points along the perimeter, dead and sometimes missing a few of their parts, as a warning to other potential intruders. That was part of Mr. Skin's big plan too. He like to keep his Crips occupied—but he also liked them to keep their *edge*.

''Shit. We're gonna get caught. I just fuckin' *know* it.'' Li'l Man paced nervously along the fence that enclosed the store's side yard, which was a jumble of old tires and what trash the powerful Southwestern winds had blown in over two years. He clutched his assault rifle by the barrel. ''You know what Mr. Skin'll do to us if he catches us doin' shit?''

''Heyyyy.'' Tino let the word out slow and easy, in its own cloud of blue smoke. His own rifle was leaned against the tires beside him. ''We're Crips, dude. It's like our privilege to choke a little rope once in a while.''

''Not when we're on watch, man. Mr. Skin don't like nobody doin' nothin' on watch.''

Tino shook his head. ''Who's gonna catch us? Everybody's over on the east side lookin' out for this robot dude. Nobody got time for our shit down here on Sixth Street.''

''They say that Steele's a pretty bad dude.''

''Nah.'' Tino took another toke. ''He comes here, we kick his ass for him. *Righteous*.''

Li'l Man came back and hunkered down next to Tino, his handkerchief headband hanging in his eyes, his assault rifle across his thighs. It was an old-fashioned design, with the magazine up front of the grip, but like almost all firearms these days it used caseless ammunition. Extruded brass for cartridges was an expensive luxury in this world of diminished expectations. Caseless ammo was lighter and more compact, the actions designed to take it mechanically simpler—no spent casings to extract. Tino and Li'l Man's weapons were Argentinean knockoffs of Israeli Galil SARs, rechambered and rebarreled to take the newer, smaller caliber ammunition.

Tino rolled himself a new number, lit it, offered it to his buddy, who waved him off irritably. Tino shrugged and said, "All the more for me, man," and thought about how the locusts hadn't come on yet this year.

Li'l Man jumped up, did a sort of broken field shuffle, toes *left*, toes *right*, poking the night with his imitation Galil.

"What the fuck's the matter with you?" Tino demanded in a croak.

"I heard something, man. I heard something."

"Bull-fucking-shit."

"*There!* There it is again. Something back in this fuckin' yard. Something's rustling around in there."

"I don't hear nothing."

Li'l Man made a whining noise and started jittering along the front of the fence that enclosed the junk-filled yard. Tino shook his head.

"Stupid fool," he said, and took a hit. When he glanced around again his partner had vanished around the corner of the yard.

Tino blew smoke and watched the Christ of the Sandias change colors, red, white, green. He heard a brief scuffling sound from his left. "Li'l Man," he said, "what you getting into?"

His answer was a wordless high-pitched sound. He frowned and climbed unsteadily to his feet, knocking over his rifle with a clatter as he did so.

"Li'l Man? What's going on? You fuckin' me, man, it's your *ass*."

His partner came around the corner. He had his hands over his ears as if trying to blot out an unbearable sound, and a horrible look on his face.

"Li'l Man," Tino said in disgust, "what the fuck—"

He saw there was somebody standing behind his partner. Some*thing*—something that glinted like metal in the starlight. Something whose hands gripped the sides of Li'l Man's head, beneath the Crip's white-knuckled hands.

"*T-tino,*" Li'l Man said in a sort of whispered scream.

His head imploded.

A man-sized metal skeleton let the headless corpse fall twitching to the weed-buckled asphalt of the parking lot and stepped gingerly over it. Tino took a step back, his mouth filling with vomit.

Donovan Steele shook clots of brain from his hands. "Can we talk?" he said.

Steele slid along the back of a run-down one-story apartment. A few candles flickered behind threadbare curtains, but nobody looked out to see the metal skeleton moving noiselessly through the dark.

He stopped near a bullet-riddled dumpster, crouching so as to present a less manlike silhouette to any casual eyes that swept across him. In front of him was a small parking lot with the rusted, boxy husk of a Toyota sitting on its rims like a cicada's shed skin. A sidestreet named Fruit ran past. On the other side was the rear of the jail, a sort of angular-wave cliff slotted with narrow barred windows. Light shone from them, white and harsh. He unslung his rocket launcher and quietly began to prepare it for firing.

"Mr. Steele."

He froze. Someone was stirring in the Toyota shell. He brought up his IR sensors, saw the glow of a human-range heat signature inside the car.

You're getting careless, he chided himself. He was focused wholly on the nearness of his goal, and the car's metal—still warm from the recently set sun—had masked the lurker.

It was still no excuse to start taking things for granted.

He eased the launcher to the ground and brought up his borrowed assault rifle as a small pair of legs swung out the passenger's side, whose door had long since vanished. Then a pair of tubes protruded like insect antenna, and a small figure rocked up and forward onto them.

The figure turned to face him. It was a small man, a dwarf

maybe, with a disproportionate head and a twisted little body. Steele stared, but he kept the rifle trained.

"Christ, you are one nightmarish son of a bitch," the newcomer rasped. "Of course, I say that to the bathroom mirror each and every monkey cunt morning of the world."

He came forward with a crunch of crutchtips on gravel, practically dragging his withered legs. Steele clicked off the safety.

"Go ahead and shoot if you want to, Mr. Steele. Of course, that'll sort of fuck up the little surprise you and I went to such trouble to set up."

"Who the hell are you?" Steele asked.

"Dameron Crowe. Chief of security to City Councilor Miguel 'Mike' Aragon—a royal dipshit if ever there was one, but my boss."

"What are you doing here?"

"Waiting for you. The other assholes all had this notion that you were going to come boiling out of the Enclave, put your pointy metal head down and run straight up the street into the middle of Downtown. Kind of a goony notion, if you think about it, but when they actually get an idea, it tends to stick in their tiny minds. And, naturally, I helped it stick."

"Aragon," Steele said coolly. "Isn't he the one who served as bait in last night's little ambush?"

"You got that right, Tin Man. Over my protests."

Steele could feel his lip curl, just as if he still had one. "A humanitarian, huh?"

"Bullshit. This idea was pure cockamamie from the git-go. There's no way we're gonna be able to hold you, even if we could capture you. And the Feds are gonna give us Bo Diddley for a lump of fused nysteel. We got nothing to gain."

"So why are you helping me—if you really are."

"Call it damage control. Things are about to start shakin' in the old Duke City, and it's got dick to do with the geological indigestion out on the West Side. This was never a very *stable* system, Bunky, and you've gone and thrown it all out of true."

"My heart bleeds for you. And the Councilor."

"You ain't got no heart, pal. You got a fusion plant the size of a fuckin' cantaloupe. Look, it's like this: We did you shit. Now I'm trying to square things up. Just something to keep in mind, if any of us are here tomorrow."

"That could be a long shot," Steele said. "I still haven't decided what to do about you."

Crowe laughed. "Do what you want. I couldn't stop you. But keep in mind, I called where you'd be coming in right on the mark. If I was looking to lay more hurt on you, I could've been waiting in the car with an M–91 all cocked and locked, now, couldn't I?

"See you around." He started off, paused, glanced back. "Oh. Your pals are on the top floor. All the legitimate prisoners are down in the tank on the ground floor. Second floor's full of SWAT buttholes. 'Bout eight on duty any given time. Or do you know all this already?"

"I had an idea."

"Huh. I guess it must've felt better to squeeze it out of some poor sentry. Therapeutic, like."

He gimped off, leaving Steele looking after him.

22

The ready-squad boys on the second lockup level were just kicking back, playing a little pool and watching a little satellite on the TV when the wall blew in.

Throwing aside the spent launcher, Steele sprinted forward, the borrowed SCK 4mm slung across his back. When he hit the middle of Fruit he leaped.

The hole blown in the wall started a little over twenty feet up. Not even Steele could leap that high. He struck the wall with a jarring impact that would have slammed the breath from a breathing man. Before he began to slide he punched his right fist into the stucco wall. It sank in, stuck. He kicked his left foot into the wall, then hauled himself upward, furiously hammering his own hand and footholds.

The second of the jail's three two-tiered levels started where the third floor should have been. It was still alive with swirling smoke and dust and somebody's hoarse, sobbing shouts of agony when Steele pulled his head up to the level of the hole.

A riot shotgun poked out of the smoke and fired. The full

charge hit Steele in the face in a compact mass.

His head snapped back. By reflex he kept a one-hand hold on the jagged cement edge. He hung on for seconds on end, stunned, convinced that he must have sustained terrific damage.

After a seemingly long time it occurred to him that being blasted in the face with a twelve-gauge military magnum load hadn't *hurt*. The impact had been unpleasant. But it hadn't damaged him, hadn't even caused him pain.

He looked up. A wild-eyed man in an assault vest was leaning out of the hole, staring and pointing the shotgun at Steele. With his free hand Steele grabbed the shotgun by the barrel and pulled. The man overbalanced and cartwheeled past Steele to the sidewalk.

With a heave of the small but powerful servomotors that drove his limbs, he levered himself up and over, into the cell-block. Shouts echoed. A figure loomed in front of Steele as he tried to get his legs under him.

A burst of full-auto fire stuttered with the nasty, ear-piercing snarl of a high-velocity 4.7. A spray of bullets hit Steele in the chest. It was like being struck by a handful of fine, wind-driven hail. It had even less chance of hurting him. He shot the man with the 10mm pistol built into his arm.

The man's eyes bulged, and he staggered back several steps gasping like a beached catfish before squeezing another burst at Steele. Armor, ceramic/steel inserts tough enough to turn the 10mm ball that was all he'd been able to turn up at the Enclave. He raised his hand and shot the man through the cheek. The gunman fell back into the bars, began to sag as if he were melting inside his SWAT vest.

Steele unlimbered his SCK and took quick stock of the situation. The doors of the cells had been electronically locked open, apparently to give the guard detail freedom of movement and also, the former police lieutenant in him said, to keep the boys from getting bored and fucking around and winding up locking somebody in one of the cells about the time the hammer came down. There were six or seven men—*seven, confirmed by heat signatures and sounds. No excuse for imprecision with the senses you've got now*—scattered everywhere. Two had armored assault vests on, one was struggling into one adjusted for somebody with a smaller frame than he had, and a third was diving into the stairwell. The rest—

He held the *Shin Chuo Kogyo* in one hand and just slashed with it as if it were the hero's sword in a samurai *chanbara* epic, ripping short bursts so quickly they were almost one long one. It was approved technique for a true machine pistol—which, with his strength, the SCK was.

Men screamed and came apart in sprays of blood, shockingly bright in the hyperkinetic flicker of the fluorescent lights. The man struggling with the vest had managed to get it stuck over his head, so he got to die without having to watch.

The two who had armor on kept their feet despite body hits. Steele turned to the nearest, who was emptying his own assault rifle at Steele in a single shuddering orgasm of fire, just as the ammo indicator display on the back of the SCKs receiver flashed down to *1*.

"Shit," Steele said. He raised the weapon as though it were a pistol and shot him just to the right of the bridge of his nose. Black and red mist sprayed out behind his head.

The remaining cop finished pumping the last of his pistol magazine into Steele, threw the piece at Steele, and bolted for the stairs. Even Steele's reflexes wouldn't permit him to fish a fresh clip out of the pouch and slam it into the well before his quarry got away. Without thinking, he swooped down, picked up the eight ball the explosion had knocked off the pool table from the floor by his right foot, and threw it with a deceptively easy three-quarters-overhand motion.

It hit the fleeing man in the back of his head and crushed his skull into his medulla just as he got the heavy door open. He jerked and went flying down the steps in a spastic dance of already-dead limbs.

Steele reloaded. Moving rapidly but methodically he policed up weapons and gear. They had been well armed, these boys. Just not well enough.

Sounds from the stairs. Steele selected a fragmentation grenade from his booty, pulled the pin as he crossed to the stairwell.

He opened the door. SWAT troopers were crowding up the stairs. The lead man had just made the turn at the landing below and started up.

"Catch," Steele said. He tossed the grenade to the first man and shut the door.

Even through the heavy metal door the explosion sounded

very loud in the confines of the stairwell. Steele quickly primed
three more frag grenades and rolled them down the stairs like
so many apples on the groaning wounded. While they were
going off he pulled the pins on two tear gas grenades and a
nausea gas canister. He'd always had a great fondness for
nausea gas during his Strike Force days. A scumbag who was
hard-core enough—and they all were in no-man's-land could
blink and shrug off tear gas. *Nobody* shrugged it off when all
their guts were fighting to get out of their mouths at the same
time.

He sent those rattling down the stairs to complicate life for
the next wave of reinforcements. Then he crossed to the stairs
going up.

"*Get back!*" the SWAT sergeant screamed at the door,
clutching the detonator in both hands. The trooper on duty with
him on the third level stared at him with huge terrified animal
eyes. "*Stay back or I'll blow everybody right straight to hell!*"

The sergeant never expected to be put in the position of
actually having to *use* the detonator to set off all the charges
emplaced around the hostages, not to mention him and the sole
sad troop he had for backup. He thought he was pretty damned
hard-core. But even when he'd been assuring Spud Laurentian
that he would really truly no-fail blow himself and the captives
to smoking gobbets if the cyborg somehow got this far, he'd
been telling himself, *no way*.

But now he was thinking, *yes, I can*. Because whatever had
gone on down there on the floor below, it sounded like a horror
movie come all the hell to life. Now *Terminator Part Twenty-
Three* was clumping up the stairs after the sergeant's personal
ass, and the sergeant was thinking that at least the Thermite
and shaped charges would be *quick*.

"Get back," he said again. He heard the footsteps coming
closer. Weird clicks like some kind of giant insect might make,
ticking along on its claws. "I'm warning you! *God damn it,
stay away!*"

A fist punched through the bottom of the door. The sergeant
and his troopie looked down. It was so unexpected they didn't
react at all, other than to gape.

The hand dropped something on the cement floor and with-
drew. Sergeant and trooper looked at each other, then stared

back down at the object, trying to make sense of it all.

The stun grenade went off. Its incredibly intense flash and loud bang were supposed to blind and befuddle enemy troops. It worked. The sergeant was standing there with his detonator forgotten in his hand, trying to blink away huge fat purple after-image balloons when Donovan Steele came through the door and killed him and the trooper with precisely placed single shots.

"Steele!" Jilly cried, throwing herself at the bars like a lemur.

"You are taking a foolish risk in coming here," said Dr. Singh.

"I'm thrilled you're so glad to see me, doctor."

"This is a substantial risk even for you. You may be immune to small-arms fire, but our hosts have been bragging about how many anti-tank weapons they possess."

"I don't necessarily see myself as having that much to lose, doctor."

"Be careful," Jilly said. "They've got anti-tank charges and Thermite wired up all over the place."

"So I see," Steele said, scanning the two-story chamber. "Probably tamper-proofed to keep me from disarming them."

"I think so," Jilly said. "I haven't been able to examine any, close up."

"No point bothering with it. Are there controls for the cell doors up here?"

Jilly pointed to an access panel by the door. "They've been using that. But I think it's mainly meant for when they want to check individual cells during lock-down. I bet it's locked out now, and they can only open the doors down at the front desk."

"I bet you're right." He looked at her. "Where'd you learn about things like lock-downs, anyway?"

"I'm a versatile kind of girl."

"I guess." Steele peeled the panel back like the foil wrapper on a frozen dinner. The pilot lights all glowed red, and nothing happened when he pressed the buttons.

"*Okay*," he said. He walked up to Jilly's cell. She hovered there, looking as if she wanted to grab him and kiss him. He gestured her back.

He sized up the bars, then lashed a horizontal knife-hand blow. The bar on the right buckled. He nodded, hacked at the bar on the left, took three ringing cuts at the horizontal that tied them together, and held out his hand to help Jilly step primly through.

She threw herself at him, arms trapping his neck in a drowner's grip as if she never intended to let go. Instead, she released him almost at once and stepped back, pushing at her bangs where they fell in her eyes.

"All right. I know we have to move. Gee, I hope your heightened senses don't include your sense of smell; I must smell like I've been dead a week."

Next Steele battered open the bars of the cell Sally Lanz shared with fellow EMT Dave Duncan. Duncan was pale, but with Sally's help he walked out.

Steele thought Dr. Jabrandar Singh's mouth was slightly set when Steele liberated him, as if he were miffed at being last. Nonetheless when he emerged Dr. Singh took Steele's hand in a quick, firm shake, nodded his turbaned, impeccable head graciously, and said, "I thank you, for myself and my people."

Then Jilly screamed, "*Look out!*" and threw a body block at Dr. Singh.

23

Steele's ultra-keen hearing caught and separated the sounds of the pistol shot and of the impact of a bullet in flesh, even though they came almost simultaneously. He spun, raising his arm with the built-in pistol.

A tall man with a grizzled flattop and a paunch contained by an armored assault vest stood at the door to the cells. As Steele spun he lowered his own pistol and held up his left hand to show Steele what was in it.

"Dead man switch. Anything happens to me and all this goes up in one big white flash. And even if we've misjudged and it doesn't take you down, your friends burn."

"Stalemate," Steele said. He glanced back. Dr. Singh was sitting against the bars of a cell. The left side of his shirt was soaked in blood. He seemed to be alive, and both Jilly and Sally were tending to him.

"Not exactly. All's I have to do is step back behind the door here, relax my hand, and watch the fireworks through the bulletproof glass. But I got a different proposition for you. I'm

Spud Laurentian, by the way. Ex-Federal substance and practices enforcement.''

"I'm not really pleased to meet you."

Laurentian wrinkled his face around an aw-shucks grin. Two SWAT troopers in full battle gear complete with Kevlar helmets and blackened Lexan visors stepped in and took up positions flanking him. A third man came in wearing a welder's metal mask and dragging a portable arc-welding unit.

"What happens now is you get welded good and solid to the bars in here. And we strap a neat little shaped charge to the middle of your ribcage, with an electronic detonator rigged so that if you actually break the welds, and break contact with the bars, it blows you in half. Neat, huh?"

Steele said nothing.

Laurentian brandished the deadman detonator again. "Or you can just say no. Then you burn, she burns, everybody burns."

"You saw *Heavy Metal?*" Jilly gasped in disbelief.

"Hey, little lady," Laurentian said defensively, "I was young once too. I was a real hell-raiser in my time, you better believe it."

"Yeah. I bet you were a holy terror in the locker room. I bet nobody ever bent over to pick up the soap when you were in the showers."

Laurentian's face purpled. He glared at Steele. "Well, hero? What's it gonna be?"

For a long moment Steele stared at him. Then he stepped back against the bars of an undamaged cell.

The man with the arc welder bustled forward. "Hold your arm up here, please. Straight out from the shoulder, forearm vertical along the bar."

"I could grab you for a hostage, you know," Steele said to him.

"Ah, that wouldn't do nobody no good. Old Spud would never negotiate."

"Fuckin'-A," Laurentian said.

The tech hesitated, and Steele saw his eyes flicker behind the smoke-stained goggles. He had apparently been thinking that was a bluff, a negotiating ploy, that good ol' Spud wouldn't *really* melt him along with the hostages.

Laurentian read his body language. "Snap it up here, Harry.

Don't go getting any ideas about balking here. I know where to find your wife and kids.''

Steele held his arm as Harry directed. ''Don't let him do this,'' Jilly begged. ''He's never going to let us go.''

Laurentian smirked. ''Do you want to trade a possibility for a certainty, Steele? You know I won't hesitate to—*whoa!*'' He jumped in the air and spun his head around.

Bowling Harry over, Steele crossed the open floor in three quick strides. With surprising quickness, the heavyset former Fed was turning back around when Steele wrapped a nysteel claw around the hand that held the detonator and squeezed.

Laurentian screamed. Blood squirted in ten-foot arcs. The detonator transmitter was robust, like all modern grown-circuit electronics, but died without a peep as it was crushed along with the bones of Laurentian's hand.

Steele caught a glimpse of the diminutive form of Dameron Crowe standing behind Laurentian in the open door. He was still holding up the crutch he'd used to goose the ex-Fed.

The SWAT trooper to Laurentian's left had simply frozen. He was still standing with his assault rifle pointed into the room when the back of Steele's right fist slammed against the side of his head. The Kevlar buckled but prevented the blow from staving in his skull. It didn't prevent the force of the blow from snapping his neck.

The other armored cop wheeled and fired a burst into Steele's ribs. Ricocheting bullets whined through the block. Steele pivoted and gave him a straight right to the center of the visor.

The tough polymer faceplate shattered. The trooper dropped. The hand Steele drew back dripped blood.

''There's a truck waiting out back where you came in,'' Dameron Crowe said. ''It's not gonna be quite so easy getting out as it was getting in.''

Steele looked at the man and wished he could sigh. ''Thanks.'' He looked to his friends. ''How's the doctor?''

Singh was standing up, waving off the helping hands and wincing in pain. ''Mobile, Mr. Steele. Fortunately the chest is mostly air.''

''If your lung doesn't collapse,'' Dave said.

''I have another. Now we must hurry, as the . . . gentleman said.''

There was a muffled *crump* from somewhere and the bars vibrated. Crowe's eyebrows shot up.

"Mortar," he said. "Looks like some of your bozo friends in the Enclave found some balls in their pants after all and are putting on a diversion. Better haul dick. It's *still* not gonna be easy."

"How are *you* going to get out?" Steele asked.

Crowe laughed. "Same way I came in. Waltz right past the guards." He vanished with startling alacrity.

Steele gestured for the others to come on. Jilly yelled his name.

He turned. From being slumped against the wall by the door cradling his pulped hand to his chest, Spud Laurentian had launched himself into a quick dive for his fallen sidearm.

Steele was quicker. His skeletal foot pinned Laurentian's left wrist with his fingers wiggling like pale beetle legs millimeters from the Pachmayr grip of the pistol.

Steele bore down. Wristbones powdered. Laurentian howled. Steele hauled him up by the collar and propelled him into the middle of the rec area. He hit the pool table and collapsed.

An armored trooper was emerging from the far stairwell as Steele reached the second level. Steele shot him in the legs. The next man crouched behind his writhing form. Measuring the shot with his sighting lasers, Steele gave him a three-round burst right in the faceplate. His visor held, but the head went away anyway.

Steele underhanded a frag grenade into the doorway. Jilly and Sally popped out of the door behind him with the assault rifles recovered from Laurentian's fallen escorts at the ready.

Steele tossed Jilly the sack he'd improvised from the undershirt of one of the men he killed on the way in. It contained the rest of the liberated grenades.

"Keep them busy on the stairs while I take a look outside."

She nodded and ran for the stairs with Sally right behind. Steele moved to the opening his rocket had made and looked out.

A bullet ricocheted off a cement edge right by where he was used to his ear being. He jerked back, then thought, *what the hell?* He wasn't going to be needing those reflexes quite so much any more.

He stepped boldly into the opening. As promised, there was a truck, an open-topped carryall, parked just below. Steele could see maybe a dozen people on the street, Crips, Council gunmen, a couple of armored SWAT troopers. Some of them were pointing off to the east. Steele could hear the *pop-pop* of a firefight coming from that direction.

At least half a dozen guns opened up on him at once. He stood there with small caliber bullets clattering all around him, bouncing off his ribs and thighbones and even his face, picking off the shooters one by one.

His peripheral vision was one of the few faculties that had been weakened by the loss of the organic part of him. When somebody fired an M-91 from somewhere east along the street, it was only the distinctive whoosh and white smoke puff of the launch that alerted him in time.

He threw himself flat back, catching his nysteel skull a nasty crack on the cement floor. The rocket buzzed in through the opening to explode in a brilliant white fan against the bars of a cell on the second tier.

"Everybody okay?" he yelled.

"We're fine," Sally shouted back. "But we're running low on grenades."

Steele took a second to reload, then came up firing. He had registered exactly where the rocket had come from: behind an Audi sedan parked across the intersection. The rocket man was hidden, hunkered down to prep a second round.

Steele picked out the place where he knew the gas tank was, locked in with his lasers and fired short bursts until the fuel blew with a whoomp. The explosion didn't set the rocketeer on fire, but did send him—her—scuttling frantically backward across the intersection on her ass. She turned and got up to scramble away, still dragging her fresh launcher by the sling. Steele dropped her with a burst.

A blast of machinegun fire shit him in the chest. This wasn't any penny-ante 4.7mm squad automatic; it was full-dress 7.62, and it sent him sprawling.

"I don't want to be a pest," asked Dave Duncan, who was crouched with his back to the door of a cell near the hole clutching Laurentian's 9mm, "but how are we going to get *down?*"

"Improvise a rope or something out of clothes," Jilly called. She flipped a nausea-gas grenade into the stairwell and hurriedly pulled the door shut.

"Will that work? Won't the knots come untied?"

"You have a better idea?" Steele asked. He picked himself up.

This time he approached the hole from the side, cautiously. He stuck his head around for a by-the-book three-second look.

It was all the time he had before another burst roared at him from the apartments on the other side of Fruit. He jerked back in time to avoid this one. 7.62 couldn't hurt him any more than the lighter stuff, but he didn't have time to keep getting hosed off his feet like a slapstick clown.

This time he had spotted the flare of the weapon. He had also made a holographic picture of the gun's barrel and the operator's face half-hidden behind the receiver, complete with precise range and bearings. He composed himself for a moment.

He pivoted, brought his rifle to his shoulder, fired once. The machinegun went silent. He watched a moment longer, scanning the window with lasers and IR, in case an assistant gunner made a move to take over the MG. Nobody moved.

He surveyed the street. There were still forms sprawled everywhere. Everyone who could still move had evidently decided to do so. Nothing like a figure straight out of a nightmare that could stand there with bullets bouncing off it and systematically and inevitably gun you down with single shots to power down morale.

"Ready to go?" he asked.

Dave and Sally were just finishing knotting together their pale green smocks and trousers, Dr. Singh's now-bloodstained suitcoat, and various items of clothing hurriedly stripped from the dead. That was a fortunate trait of EMTs: They weren't squeamish about handling dead people, even the very messily dead.

Sally Lanz tied one end around her waist and sat down with her feet braced against the wall at the bottom of the hole. "Jilly, you're first," Steele said.

Jilly slung her assault rifle, took a turn of the makeshift

"rope" under the armpits, and rappelled expertly down the back wall of the jail. There was an eight-foot drop at the bottom. She let go of the rope, landed lightly, and ran to cover behind the carryall to cover.

Steele slipped back to cover the stairwell. He could hear voices encouraging each other at the bottom. Nobody seemed eager to advance. The foot of the stairs was kind of blockaded by the dead and the wounded, who were being noisy, and who could blame them? Also the going was slippery with blood and spilled organic parts.

Dr. Singh went out next, then Dave. Steele dropped his final two grenades down the stairs just as a wave of reinforcements started up and ran.

Sally was standing by the hole in her underwear, still holding the dubious rope around her waist. "How do we work this?" she asked.

Steele picked up her rifle, slung it over his shoulder, and grabbed the free end. "Go for it." She nodded and climbed out the window. Not bothering to belay, Steele just played out the rope, lowering her.

Halfway down the rope unraveled. Sally plummeted. She rolled like a paratrooper when she hit, but Steele heard her ankle pop.

The door banged open behind him. He grabbed his own rifle and fired a long burst, driving back the first men out the door. Wearing armor still didn't mean it was fun to be shot.

A SWAT trooper shouldered his way to the front and went to one knee, leveling an M-91 right at Donovan Steele's chest.

"Where'd he get that?" somebody screamed.

His comrades lunged at him. "*Don't shoot that in here, you stupid son of a bitch—*"

Steele turned and jumped as the man fired.

24

The SWAT troopers screamed as the launcher's backblast scorched them. The rocket buzzed over Steele's head and neatly severed a light standard over on Lomas.

Steele landed much harder than Sally had, but it was the cement sidewalk that cracked, not his nysteel ankles.

Dr. Singh and Dave Duncan were helping Sally into the vehicle. Dave slid behind the wheel. The bandages which were his sole upper garment were soaked with fresh blood that glistened in the moonlight.

"You're hurt," Jilly said to him.

"I'll hurt a lot worse if we get caught here. I'm still the best driver, except maybe Steele—and it looks as if he has better things to do!"

It was true. Fresh waves of attackers poured out around both ends of the block.

Steele glanced quickly left, letting his fire-control systems get a fix on the locations and approximate vectors of the nearer attackers. He took Sally's assault rifle in his left hand and let the computer inside his skull fire it for him full-auto while he turned his head right and used his sighting lasers to quickly engage and hit individual targets. Behind cover or out in the open didn't matter—at this range, under fifty meters, if they exposed enough of themselves to see what they were shooting at, he could nail them dead to rights.

It occurred to him that he had, after all, always used his well-trained body and mind as a precision fighting instrument. He could appreciate the advantages to being a true cyborg— or maybe a killer robot pretending it was a cyborg. Being stripped of his flesh, it seemed, had liberated him to bring his mind and skills into fuller harmony with the mechanical and cybernetic systems that supported him.

He still wasn't sure he wanted to live that way.

The attackers to the east fell back or went to ground, cowering with terror lest they leave some part of their bodies exposed to that inexorable killing machine. He looked west, toward Fifth Street. His fire in that direction had been accurate enough to cut down three Crips and a Council patrolman, and Jilly, adding her own fire, had accounted for two more. Several were shooting at her from cover; Steele dropped one and the others fled.

"Jesus," Dave yelled, "let's blow this pop stand!"

Steele vaulted into the back of the vehicle. It peeled away in a squeal of tires.

Miguel "Mike" Aragon lay behind sandbags on the more-than-incipient paunch he was so self-conscious about and thought, not without guilt, that he'd never had more fun in his life.

He held a pistol, an actual devil-incarnate 9mm *hand gun* that Dameron Crowe had insisted he take with him, out in front of him at the full extension of both arms. Every time there was a lull in firing from across the tracks he would raise up a fraction and blast off another twenty-round magazine into the night.

He was glad he and his troops had held position after the mystery explosion twenty minutes ago, off beyond the Civic Plaza somewhere. Otherwise he would have missed the Enclave attack completely. And he wouldn't have missed it for the world.

He was dug in out in front of the old Sunshine Building, which was in about its eighth incarnation as an old-movie house. His position covered the underpass where Central burrowed briefly below the railroad tracks. Nobody had actually dared trying to come through there yet. He hadn't actually seen anyone at all, only the occasional firefly flash of shots coming in from across the tracks. None of his own people had been hit, as far as he could tell, and he had no illusions that he or any of his men had actually hit anything themselves.

But that was fine. This was *fun*. He didn't really mean to hurt anyone anyway. He had only discovered the great truth that it was fun to point a gun and make it go bang.

Firing faded. He pushed his pistol over the top of the sandbags and let another magazine go, pumping his chubby trigger finger for all he was worth.

"Wow," he said, dropping back to the comforting shelter of the sandbags. He set about trying to remember how to get the old magazine out and the new one in.

Lying on their flat sports-coated bellies behind him, Dwight and Tay exchanged glances. There was shooting going on to both sides now, making plenty of racket.

It was as good a time as any.

They stood up. Their Smith & Wesson .40 caliber semiautos came out of their shoulder holsters. They aimed.

Aragon caught the motion from the corner of his eye and looked around. "Say, guys, can either of you tell me . . . say, what are you *doing*?"

"Sorry it had to be this way, Mike," Dwight said.

"Nothing personal, man," said Tay. "It's been real."

Miguel "Mike" shut his eyes. He heard a pop.

He was feeling a marked sense of anticlimax—a shot that ended a life as sensitive and caring as his had been should make a lot more impressive sound than "pop"—when it occurred to him that he hadn't actually *felt* anything. He wasn't sure that this was right. *I've always heard you never hear the shot that kills you,* he thought, *but not to* feel *it?*

He opened his eyes. Dwight was standing staring straight ahead, with his eyes bugged out farther than Aragon had ever seen human eyes go. He fell forward like a Ponderosa pine felled by loggers.

Tay spun. Dameron Crowe stood right behind him. The tip of his right crutch was smoking. It was also pointed straight at the bridge of Tay's narrow WASP nose.

"I always knew you two wimps were dirty," Crowe said. "Enjoy Hell, yuppie scum."

He shot Tay between the eyes and looked admiringly at the tip of his crutch. "Good old .22 long rifle," he said. "Not much stopping power, but it's fine for plain old-fashioned murder."

"They were going to kill me," Aragon said wonderingly.

"No shit, Sherlock."

"Why?"

"Somebody paid them to, I expect."

"Who'd do a thing like that?"

"Do you want that list alphabetically or in order of probability? It's kind of a tie for first, now that I think about it. I can think offhand of four other City Councilors, your loving dyke wife Janis, and one prominent local civic and gang leader who wanna see you croaked. Some people at the Enclave don't love you much either by now, but they haven't had time to rig something like this.

"That reminds me."

He turned, letting his right elbow take his weight on the brace of his crutch while he rummaged in the side pocket of his plaid sports jacket. He came out with the detonator-transmitter the sergeant on guard over the hostages had carried. Crowe had snagged it while everyone was looking at Dr. Singh.

"Got just a few loose ends to tie up," he said, and pointed the device toward the jail.

"Come on, Coach," Spud Laurentian gasped, dragging himself toward the door on his elbows. It had been the longest journey of his life, and now he had almost made it. "Just a few more feet, Coach, you can do it."

That evil little fuck Crowe was going to eat some heavy shit before he died for poking him in the fanny like that. Spud Laurentian was good at making people eat shit. Federal agents kind of got the knack.

Singh, too, and that Romero girl with the tight little butt—he was sorry he'd interrupted his boss earlier. He should have let DiStefano go ahead and dick the little bitch. They should have just *made* time.

And Steele. *Lieutenant* Donovan Steele. What a joke. He might be made of super-resistant polymerized alloy, but he could still feel pain. That he had come at all—and surrendered meekly when his little pals were put in jeopardy—showed that.

He'd been right about Steele. He'd been right all along. The man was a pussy. He had let Laurentian *live*.

There—the door handle had finally come into reach. Agonizingly, Spud climbed to his feet. He leaned forward to work the handle with his elbow.

"Steele!" he screamed. "I'm down but I'm not out, you motherfucker. I'm going to show you a *whole world* of hurt! I—"

The room went white around him.

Firing over the tail of the carryall, Steele saw the top floor of the jail blow out with a brilliant flash and an eruption of dust.

"Hold on, everybody," Dave called, "we're at the wire."

He hit the accelerator. The thin barbed-wire strands parted with a squeal and musical ping.

Jilly Romero reared up from her prone firing position in the vehicle's rear and shook a fist. "All right, you bastards, we're out of there!"

From the big checkpoint at Lomas and First Street a machinegun spoke. Bullets whanged off Steele's nysteel bones. Jilly started to fly over the side.

"*Cory!*" Steele screamed, flashing back to the terrible instant when police bullets cut his teenaged daughter down by flamelight. He caught the young woman with a desperate grab and pulled her back.

The carryall flashed across Lomas and to safety behind the cover of the buildings on Fifth Street. The damage was already done.

Jilly had taken at least three rounds through the chest. Blood bubbled from her mouth and nostrils.

"Well," she said, "at least this way you won't have to rescue me any more."

She closed her eyes.

Steele put his head back and howled like a wolf.

_EPILOGUE_____

Donovan Steele sat on the roof of the Medical Center gazing in an unfocused way at the distant Christ of the Sandias, still a few hours from coming on. He was trying not to think at all, but he couldn't help seeing the faces. Cory, Dev Cooper, Raven, Ice—Jilly. Everyone he cared for he'd gotten killed.

He heard footsteps behind him. One set he recognized as belonging to a tall woman who was walking with difficulty—Janet Virág, up and around and toting, an electrical bone-growth stimulator to help her shattered femur knit. It wasn't that big a surprise; doctors of the day liked to get patients active as soon as possible, and Dr. Singh was a particular believer in it. He himself had refused to lose any time to his own chest wound.

Besides, Virág had hiked three miles against the sluggish Río Grande current with her bullet wounds and busted leg. Within thirty-six hours of the ambush she had been in a wheel-chair, alternately defending her security kids for launching an impromptu diversionary attack in support of Steele and reaming

her security kids out for abandoning their posts. She was a
hard one to keep down.

Someone was helping her, though—or she was helping
someone, more likely. That someone was younger, smaller,
and also female, walking with difficulty but not limping. It
almost sounded like—

No, he told himself firmly. *Don't even start. You can torture
yourself into madness all too easily. You don't have Dev to
talk you back any more.*

"Aren't you even going to say hi?" Jilly Romero asked.

Steele turned. She was standing there looking drawn and
disheveled in a light hospital robe, leaning on Virág, who was
leaning on a massive cane.

He jumped to his feet. "Jilly! I thought—" He shook his
head. "I *didn't* think. You were dead. Sally pronounced you
dead before we got back to the Enclave."

She nodded. "I was dead, all right. It just didn't take."

"They hyperoxygenated her and shot her full of thromboxane
suppressants and stuff," Virág said. "There wasn't really any
brain cell loss. She came back fine; she's a strong little shit."

He just stood there looking at her, not yet daring to believe.
"But it was just two days ago—"

"Another miracle of modern medical science," Virág said.
"You should know all about that stuff."

She came to him on her own power, stood on tiptoe, kissed
his bare death's head grin without hesitation or self-conscious-
ness.

"I'm still a little fragile, so I can't hug you," she said. Then
she grabbed him by the bare bones of his forearm.

"Come on," she said.

"Where are we going?"

"I want to give you a present."

"What is it?"

She looked at him, and her eyes glowed like polished amber.
"You're going to have to trust me."

He felt the kiss on his lips and opened his eyes.
Opened his eyes.

Jilly's face was inches from his and rising. She smiled.
"Welcome back."

He smiled. It changed to a frown; something was partially

obscuring the lower middle section of his vision. He reached up and felt it with his fingers.

It was a nose. Warm and pliable.

Then he noticed his hand. It was pink and complete, not skeleton metal.

He shot upright. *"What have you done to me?"*

"Oh, dear," Dr. Eleanor Ngoya said from the hospital room door. "I hope we haven't made a mistake."

"We have given you your body back," Dr. Singh said from beside her. "If that displeases you we could relieve you of it again, I suppose."

Steele was sitting with his legs over the edge of the bed, feeling himself all over.

"How?"

"Dr. Ngoya's marvelous vats, of course. Really, you might thank her."

"There aren't any samples of my tissue anywhere. How could you do—" He held a hand before his face, rotated it wonderingly. "—this."

"For that you have the indefatigable Ms. Romero to thank," Dr. Singh said.

He looked at her. She was practically glowing with pleasure.

"What is he talking about?" he asked.

She held out a twisted wisp of cloth. He accepted it, untwisted it, peered at what looked like a tiny shred of dried meat inside.

"I collected it off you when I was cleaning you up, back in the shed in Mt. Zion," Jilly said breathlessly. "I *thought* it looked like tissue. I saved it and brought it all the way back with me."

"It does not seem particularly large, Lieutenant," Dr. Ngoya said, pronouncing it *leftenant*. "But in fact it was more than ample for us to get a complete undisturbed sequence of your DNA and confirm it a million times over."

"Even in this day and age that takes a pretty piece of computer time," Jilly said.

Ngoya nodded. She seemed almost as excitement-flushed as Jilly.

"After that, it was all fairly simple, really, even though we've never done such a comprehensive regeneration before. There is one thing I must warn you of, Lieutenant: For a few days you're going to be your own worst enemy."

He laughed. The sound of his own voice startled him. "That's nothing new."

"You must understand, we don't have the technology to restore the bullet-resistant artificial skin you had before. What you have is simply skin, your own skin. You're liable to bruise yourself a great deal until you become accustomed to it."

"You still have a nysteel skeleton, Lieutenant," Dr. Singh said. "We can do marvelous things with bones and joints, as Ms. Virág can attest, but we could not regenerate an entire new skeleton for you. Something else to keep in mind is that, while your muscles have been built up through chemical and electrical stimulation, they are not fully toned. You of course have the same great strength and speed your powered skeleton gave you."

He touched his temples, felt hair there. "What about . . . what about my brain?" It sounded melodramatic, but he had to ask.

Dr. Ngoya looked crestfallen. "We don't have the facilities to upload and download personalities; your Project Download was not exactly forthcoming with technical information."

"So I'm still . . ."

"You are still a human personality surviving in a mechanical matrix." Steele felt a twinge at the word. "As to the metaphysical implications of that fact, I am incompetent to speculate."

"Go look at yourself," Jilly urged.

He stood, weaved slightly, walked to the sink. It felt as if his skeleton was in danger of cutting through the balls of his feet. Having skin was going to take some getting used to.

His image struck him like a slap. The same rugged face, the same gray eyes.

Jilly laid a hand on his arm. "You know, you are kind of handsome, in an alarming kind of way."

It all hit him then. He turned and raced for the bathroom and threw his guts up in the toilet.

Nothing had ever felt better in his life.

Steele and Jilly stood on the edge of the erstwhile golf course and watched the sun fall behind the volcanoes.

"So what are you going to do now?" she asked, her voice

studiously neutral. "Are you still going to Los Alamos?"

He shrugged. "I don't know. Right now I'm trying to adjust to having my own flesh back." He gave her a grin. "Thanks again, by the way. I owe you a lot."

"Looks like a small payment for repeatedly saving my life," she said. She slipped her arm into his. "What will you do, then?"

"I'm still up in the air. It looks as if you'll need some help around here for a while—the City Council isn't real happy with you or me right now. I feel obligated to lend a hand if they try something else. I was the one who brought them down on your necks, after all.

"After that—I need to find out what happened to Matrix. My electronic twin, my . . . brother."

"I know. You told me."

He nodded. "I'm worried. I don't see how anything *could* have happened to him, but I should have heard from him. On the other hand, I don't have the first idea of how I'm going to look for him. So it's not as if I'm about to rush off or anything."

The sun had burst and bled red and orange all over the horizon. A pocket-sized burrowing owl flew up out of its burrow in the cutbank and perched on the limb of a nearby elm to scrutinize the humans with round critical eyes.

Jilly laid her head on Steele's shoulder. "So you won't be leaving for a while."

He stroked her hair. "No," he said, "not for a while."

It was nine in the morning, but the day got hot quickly this time of year. The verti from Los Alamos finished its gentle glide by rotating its wings vertical, flaring, and landing straight down in a pool of mercury sun-shimmer in front of Kirtland Base's main hangar.

Five-foot-eight, black, and round of face, shoulder, and belly, Major General Paul Whiteman strode forward with all the authority he could muster as the tilt-rotor craft's door opened and a ladder folded down. At his side walked Colonel George Donelson, his brisk stride, immaculate uniform, and cool expression behind dark aviator's glasses a reproach to the sweat already starting to trickle from beneath the bill of the general's cap and blunt the edges of the creases in his uniform trousers. The colonel was a runner, a hard charger, a man of action.

General Whiteman was a more contemplative type. But still, a leader of men, and conscious of the role he ought to play.

A man in a white suit and Panama hat came down the ladder, followed by a woman with long dark hair. Her silk blouse, black splashed with red and white, and baggy olive drab trousers with many pockets molded themselves fleetingly to her slim form in very intriguing ways as the downdraft of the slowing rotors battled the ceaseless desert wind.

"I'm Major General Whiteman," the general said, shaking hands with the man in white. The newcomer's grasp was limp and cold as a piece of sushi. "Welcome to Albuquerque, doctor, ma'am."

The woman gave him a half-smile and nodded but didn't offer her hand. Whiteman didn't dream of thrusting his upon her, just as he didn't dream of giving into his urge to wipe his hand on his trousers after her companion's handshake. The general was a gentleman of the old school.

Colonel Donelson wasn't. He didn't have time for niceties. There was the small matter of crushing a rebellious city waiting.

"So where's this secret weapon you promised us, Doctor James?" he demanded. "The one that's going to take down this Steele character and bring the City Council and the gangs to heel?"

The woman took off her aviator glasses—she looked better in them than the colonel did, and better still without them— and swept her surroundings with a smoky blue-gray gaze that took in the desert, the volcanoes, the clustered buildings of Downtown, and finally Colonel Donelson.

"I'm it," she said, and smiled a beautiful smile.